HIGH HAWK

HIGH HAWK

Amy Frykholm

UNIVERSITY OF IOWA PRESS | IOWA CITY

University of Iowa Press, Iowa City 52242

Copyright © 2024 by Amy Frykholm

uipress.uiowa.edu

Printed in the United States of America

Cover design by Brad Norr

Text design and typesetting by April Leidig

Printed on acid-free paper

Library of Congress Cataloging-in-Publication Data

Names: Frykholm, Amy Johnson, 1971– author.

Title: High Hawk / Amy Frykholm.

Description: Iowa City: University of Iowa Press, 2024.

Identifiers: LCCN 2024004754 (print) | LCCN 2024004755 (ebook) |

ISBN 9781609389734 (paperback; acid free paper) |

ISBN 9781609389741 (ebook)

Subjects: LCGFT: Fiction. | Novels.

Classification: LCC PS3606.R95 H54 2024 (print) |

LCC PS3606.R95 (ebook) | DDC 813/.6—dc23/eng/20240212

LC record available at https://lccn.loc.gov/2024004754

LC ebook record available at https://lccn.loc.gov/2024004755

For Vera

Contents

PART I

They Are Too Sacred

WINDY CREEK RESERVATION,

SOUTH DAKOTA

1970–1983

1

The Perfect B

WHEN THE INFANT arrived on the doorstep of St. Rose Parish on the Windy Creek Reservation in South Dakota, he had been carefully arranged by an unknown person in a box marked HANDI-WIPES 40-36 COUNT PACKS. Probably, they later reasoned, the box had been taken from behind the hospital near the dumpster. He lay on Styrofoam packing peanuts and was wrapped in several of the thin cotton blankets given to mothers with newborns at the Windy Creek Hospital.

Father Joe found him. He'd come down from the rectory after his morning shave and coffee, hooking his collar as he walked over frozen mud. He was a big man who rambled like a bear—a little off balance, but not without purpose. In his head, he was deeply engaged in conversation with Father Fabian, the principal of the reservation school, about a problem he hoped the man would address. He had tried this speech out directly to Father Fabian and hadn't gotten it right. Now he was endlessly revising, trying again and again. It was important, extremely important, but whenever he approached the man, whether in reality or in his head, he didn't get it right. His words fell flat. They had no effect.

When he saw the box, he couldn't immediately connect it with the squall—the sound of righteous need and sudden loss.

He carried the box into the church, and only once in his office did he lift the child out of the box and try, in an awkward way, to soothe him. Then he reached for the phone and called Alice. "Please come," he said without giving more detail. "It's a little more than I can handle."

While he waited for Alice, Father Joe tried out what few words of baby-calming he knew. "Shh, shh," he said, and bounced up and down on the balls of his Florsheims. He felt overwhelming gratitude at the sight of Alice's Plymouth on the road. Mass was starting in fifteen minutes. True, the crowd would be small on a Tuesday, and everyone would understand if they had to wait, but Father Joe liked a nice, efficient morning mass so people could get on with their day. It was a gift to the parish, a Christian duty executed. But he did wonder sometimes where he had gotten this idea. It was at odds with the people who came to mass who weren't in any kind of a hurry. They didn't have important offices to run off to or jobs that required them to be there at 9:00 sharp or long commutes through city traffic. They were gentle and somewhat slow-moving compared to the people in his first parish, who were always running around and getting things done. In truth, not one of St. Rose's people cared what time mass started or ended. The time was something that he kept in his mind, as if it mattered, as if he were still negotiating with those other people, long ago and far away.

When Alice arrived in a worn parka and snow boots, she didn't immediately relieve Father Joe of his burden as she swept into his office. She took in Father Joe by the window with the baby in his arms, still screaming insistently, and gestured with a long, elegant hand at the box.

"Is this how the baby arrived?"

He nodded.

She dug around in the box and pulled out a bottle of infant formula.

"Father Joe," she looked up, alarmed. "This milk is still warm. Did you see anyone?"

He shook his head. He couldn't remember if he had even looked. He tried, and failed, to imagine where a new mother might have heated up milk before bringing the child to the church steps. The church was on a bit of a hill, a sharp climb up from the highway, with the rectory another bit of a climb behind that. Windy Creek started in the hills behind the rectory and then wound down past the church before taking a sharp bend south and lolling peacefully toward the bluffs. It joined the Snake River and disappeared eventually into the Missouri somewhere near the border with Nebraska. There weren't many places near the church to heat milk if you didn't have a home nearby or a car.

Alice took the child and slipped the nipple of the bottle into his mouth. They both stared intently at the baby while he first resisted then relaxed. Liquid spooled around his mouth, and he made tiny sounds of pleasure. In a few moments, he had eaten and fallen asleep.

Father Joe looked at his watch. "I've got a couple of minutes before mass," he said. Alice turned to look at him sharply; her beaded earrings caught the light as she swerved. He felt embarrassed.

"That wasn't the right thing to say, was it?"

She ignored him as she placed the baby on the worn couch and, with a mother's practiced hand, refolded and tightened the blankets around him. Then she peered into the box and moved the peanuts around.

She drew out a piece of torn notebook paper, the rough edges of the spiral still on it. In blue ink, in a precise, feminine hand, there was a note. "His name is Bernard," it said. "I know you can help him."

Alice stared at the note. "That looks like mission school hand-writing," she said. "Nun-trained."

"How can you tell?"

"Look at that B," she said. "It's too perfect."

Father Joe stared at the note, trying to see what Alice saw. Then he sat down at his desk. Alice picked up the baby and held him. As he reached toward the phone, she took two swift steps across the room and put her hand on his arm.

"Don't call, Father," she said. "He's one of ours. I know it. Maybe we can find his mother ourselves, and we can help her."

Father Joe looked at her warily. She had four children of her own. The youngest, a girl named Jackie, was five, the oldest, Al-bert, thirteen, and they were a handful. She returned his look, straight and steady, her eyes lit like a bronze fire.

"You know what it means, once he gets written in their books," she said.

He paused. The space between them filled with a thousand unspoken words about "their books," about all the moments in the years they had known each other when he had reached for the phone and she had asked him for another way.

"I'll take him home," she said. "I'll do some asking around."

As Father Joe started the mass, the feel of the baby—part rigid, part soft—stayed with him. He understood Alice. She'd told him many times about the families she'd seen torn apart. There were few things she hated more than file folders with children's names on them, children who had been labeled but not loved.

"He's one of ours," she'd said.

Alice, with her mix of strength and elegance, her sturdy foot-wear and the delicate swing of her handmade earrings, stood between Father Joe and the reservation's world of mystery and strangeness. She was his one-woman altar guild and his rare invitation into Windy Creek's deeper life, a life that, without her, he would never even glimpse. She'd taken on his education from the first moment that they'd met, when she was a young mother and he was a young priest on his second assignment after the first in suburban Minneapolis hadn't gone so well.

She'd eyed him and then shook her head. "This place is going to eat you alive, Father." He'd laughed awkwardly. She hadn't.

The hospital said they had no record of any baby or any mother disappearing within the time frame of Bernard's birth. They advised Alice to call Child Protective Services and the Tribal Office for Children's Affairs. Blessed Sacrament Mission School likewise gave no information: No, sorry, no missing girls, no pregnant girls. No, no, they had no names to offer.

"You didn't say anything bad to those people, right?" Father Joe asked her when she reported the conversations.

"I said, 'Thank you so much,'" Alice said.

"In that tone of voice you use to tell people to go to hell?"

"Could be."

Beyond that they didn't call any authorities—tribal or federal or local or state. The tribe's leadership was in turmoil: there were stolen elections, and subtle and not-so-subtle threats issued outside tribal buildings; there was the question of federal intervention, possibly violent. Everything happening on Pine Ridge—just a few miles away—caused Father Joe to study the newspapers for hints about what wasn't being said.

Bernard became "Little Bear," and he was their secret.

On Sundays after mass, Father Joe went to see Alice and Bear. He drove out in the diocese's Buick Regal to her little house on a weedy patch along the creek. The house might once have been yellow, when the Office of Economic Opportunity built these little matchsticks, but now was a peeled gray, and sunken, with a porch that jutted out into the weeds. He made the trip ritually, but not without a kind of anxiety that he never called fear.

The thing about Alice's house, from Father Joe's perspective, was that you never knew who was going to be in it. There were always people who he didn't recognize smoking on the porch and new people in the living room, and people he was supposed to know but had forgotten standing in the kitchen. There were people who'd asked if they could park their car next to her house for a few days, and people who'd moved in and then out again. They all had names that Father Joe couldn't remember and stories that he forgot the minute he was back in the Buick.

On the other hand, Alice always welcomed him. She handed him a bowl of beans or meat soup and a piece of fry bread right away and poured a cup of coffee, and after the first wave of intimidation, he settled in. He would take Bear down to the creek to throw rocks into the water or watch him ride his tricycle in the dirt until the afternoon light faded. Later they fished or played catch.

"If Bear's mother didn't want him to be with us," Alice told Father Joe. "She would've abandoned him someplace besides a church."

Alice wasn't one to search for truth. She was more a truth shaper than a finder. She kept the note from Bernard's birth mother in a wooden box on a kitchen shelf that she called her treasure box, full of feathers and beads and little objects the children brought her. The note was a treasure, she told Bernard as he got older, because it had been written as a secret message. He had held it in his hands dozens of times, unfolded it and folded it, felt its creases, watched the words thin on the page.

And Father Joe also wasn't a truth seeker. He was more inclined to accept things as they were. Bear was safe and loved. He had a home and a mother and brothers and sisters. What was a birth certificate anyway? A piece of paper.

Secret messages were one thing Father Joe knew a lot about and lived by. People brought them to him all the time in that ritual the church called confession. He sometimes felt the words that passed through the confessional were like little folded-up pieces of paper, words that they wanted him to read and then burn. Secret keeping was a skill that he practiced regularly as a priest. They don't really prepare you for that labor in seminary. They tell you how to do it. "Say this. Ask that. Don't say this." But what they don't tell you is what to do with the accumulation of things you know, things that no one else knows, and how that piles up. No wonder people avoided him when they saw him at Willie's Market or on his way into the school. Always formal, always polite, but never intimate. At seminary, they'd never said what to do with that avoidance either, with the loneliness that accumulates like the secrets. Maybe that was different in other places. Maybe priests belonged more than they did on Windy Creek.

On Sundays, after Alice's house, Father Joe usually didn't feel like heading back to the rectory, even though he knew there would be a glass of Scotch waiting for him, as well as dinner—probably a roast with potatoes and green beans, because that's what Lydia believed a priest should eat on Sundays, and she wasn't too fond of his long visits out and about when there was a perfectly good dinner waiting for him in the rectory.

Instead he drove the Buick out of the creek bed and coaxed it along the rutted road up the hill to Gayle's house. Gayle was almost always on the porch waiting for him in a beat-up lawn chair of airy metal, oiling his pack saddles. He lived in a trailer in an expanse of tall grass that he occasionally rough cut with a machete, "when it gets so I can't see the sky that good from the porch." With an extra chair, the two of them sat and watched the evening fall.

Gayle was old, and he didn't know or care to know how old. His white hair fell to wisps on the back of his neck. His hands were rough and scarred like old bark.

For the first twelve years of his life, Gayle had spoken only the Lakota language, and he'd kept the sounds and the rhythms of it, even after he had been sent away to boarding school and then to the army. He had a lot of stories about those days that he would tell Father Joe, and Father Joe could never tell if they were true or if Gayle even wanted them to be true. He talked about the steam engine that carried him to boarding school, about the way people stared at him and how he stared back. He talked about fighting in World War I and becoming homeless afterward in what he called the "noisesome regions," until one day, he'd heard a voice on the wind, and it had said, "Go home." So he did. He'd claimed this patch of grass for his own and bought himself a couple of horses, even though all his own people were dead or gone by then.

But mostly he talked about his wife. "Fifty-six years we were together, Joe. I counted every one of them. You don't think of me as a counter, do you? But I counted. I count when it matters," he said a little defensively, as if arguing with someone who was not Joe.

In the summer, Father Joe could smell a little smoke from the porch and sometimes hear the trill of red-winged blackbirds. He could sometimes see eagles circling the tall grass at a distance. In the winter, they sat inside next to the woodstove, and Gayle would pause in his monologue to build up the fire and then settle down again.

"She was just a girl when I met her, and her father didn't like me, no sir." He chuckled and shook his head. "I can understand why. Those of us coming back from the army." He shifted in his chair and the metal creaked. "It was a rough time. A rough time. But he wasn't that good himself. They lost everything, and her parents had to move in here. We hung up a bedsheet to make a bedroom for them. Took our meals standing up or outside."

Father Joe would sometimes close his eyes and lean back in his chair, letting the rise and fall of Gayle's voice wash over him.

"I don't sleep no more. Do you sleep, Joe? I sure as heck don't. We made sure her parents took the peaceful journey to the ultimate road. We buried them the old Indian way with star blankets and the sweetgrass. I will tell you that. For him, it probably took a good while to find the right road." He chuckled again.

Gayle didn't ask many questions. He provided the evening's entertainment happily enough, but sometimes, maybe on one of the last nights of fall, when they could sit on the porch before it got too cold, Gayle looked out at the lone juniper tree growing in the field, out past the horses that he hadn't yet brought in to the ramshackle stable for the evening, and said, "What are you doing here, Joe? Where are your people?"

Father Joe knew how to answer one part of the question. "I grew up a few miles east of here," he said. "Sometimes it feels like a long way, though."

"Oh, you're from the Big Muddy. I knew that. You told me. But if I had to guess, I'd say you being here has something to do with a woman. There's almost always a woman. Or maybe you did something those old men in black didn't like. Is that it, Joe? You a rebel and you got sent into exile?"

Gayle wasn't Catholic, and he didn't want anything religious from Father Joe. The first time he had brought reserved sacrament, assuming Gayle was Catholic. Gayle had told him that the Mormons had come out to his house once when he was little, before the steam train, and the whole family had converted. He assumed his name was written in a book in Salt Lake City, and they'd had no cause to remove it. He had his horses, he said, and that was all the spirit he needed.

2

Vein of Ore

April 27, 1983

Dear Father Kreitzer,

If I remember correctly, this is your 57th birthday. Happy Birthday, Father. Must I really call you that? Father? Would it be all right if I called you Joseph? I read a small profile of you in the Midwest Catholic Reporter, "Priest in the Wilds," and it compelled me to write to you at last. I've wanted to write many times, but I've always stopped myself. It seemed improper, presumptuous, even uncouth. You have your life. I didn't want to intrude.

But now, for some reason, my sense of propriety has faded. I want to hear something from you, my old friend. So I will tell you a little about myself.

I did marry, as I said I would that day when we met for the last time. My husband's name is Darel. He was, as you guessed, one of my mother's choices. He is a decent man. We married quickly, in the summer, at his parents' house.

I felt I knew very well the transaction I was making. I could make my parents happy, leave you to your vocation, and get the inevitable over with, all with one simple action. I told myself

I was doing us both a favor. I was not going to be that girl who stole someone's vocation.

But there was one little thing I didn't factor in: life. I didn't know the first thing about it. I felt then that I had to decide things, make choices even if the array of possibilities seemed limited, and the most important thing was to make the right ones. Maybe you remember, but I was deeply annoyed with you for what seemed like a failure to make choices.

Now I don't feel so strongly about choice. Life has not exactly confirmed my choices, nor has it denied them. I've raised five children, and I did that decently well. They are all grown. The last one graduated from high school last spring. He's at the University of South Dakota. My oldest daughter has two little ones, and she lives in Sioux Falls. She and her husband both work at that new Citibank. You probably haven't heard of it out there. I can't imagine what you'd do with a credit card where you are.

We live on a piece of land in Harrisburg with corn fields to the west and a pig farm across the road to the east. To the south, a meadow, to the north, town. Town is a gas station and a bar, a Lutheran church and a Baptist one. There's no Catholic church so we go into Sioux Falls. St. Mary's.

Most days it's quiet around here. Darel goes to work. I read and I think. I used to do parish things, the Guild, Catholic Daughters, but a few weeks ago, I stepped away from all that. I am restless. I don't know what the next stage of my life holds for me.

I would welcome hearing from you. I know it is bold to say, maybe too bold, but I miss our conversations. I miss what I knew of your mind. I wonder about you out there on the plains; I wonder what you think about now. I apologize if this letter is awkward for you. I think of you often.

Sincerely,
Veronica

Veronica. Father Joe had opened the letter in his office with a heavy gold letter opener that had been given to him by his mother at his ordination. It was always in his desk, that sturdy tool, and it had seemed to him to convey a life's work. When you slit open a letter with it, you felt you were accomplishing something orderly and important. The letter opener contained his mother's pride, which also meant his mother's disappointment. It came from a time when he had been surrounded by expectation, when people said "brilliant," when Father Joe was going places and expected to do something important. There was a look in his mother's eyes that had haunted him until she died and stayed with him still. It said, "He should have been someone." That someone was not a reservation priest. The brilliant Father Joseph Kreitzer had departed this life in Minnesota, three years after seminary, when the rector of St. Martin's in Emmet Lake, the eminent William Rossling, had dismissed Father Joe wordlessly and arranged for him to take the parish of St. Rose on Windy Creek. Veronica would know nothing of this. It wasn't something the *Midwest Catholic Reporter* would have mentioned.

But that she would write to him and someday he would be sitting in his office opening a letter from her with that letter opener—he had not imagined it. His heart raced, and he worried vaguely for a moment about his health. He panicked at the thought of Alice finding him dead in his office, with this letter from Veronica in his hand. These days he thought more often of heart attacks than he ever had before.

He was surprised by the way she had brought back their final conversation. It wasn't something he often wanted to remember. He'd chosen other moments from the spring of 1951 to hold on to, moments he had repeated over and over to himself until they had become more true than the ones that she now brought up. It was a little shocking, how she had done that with so few words. He was stunned as well by the tone. He tried to name it. Anger? Bitterness? Affection? Regret? *Life has not exactly confirmed my choices.* What did that mean? The letter felt potent, as if it were carrying a sharp energy, an energy that wanted into his life.

His own visions of Veronica were different, softer, less pointed, furred over by time and sentimentality. He often pictured them walking along the Mississippi River in late fall with piles of soggy leaves everywhere and a leaden sky. He had been in seminary, writing a thesis on the psalms and studying Hebrew diligently. She had been an undergraduate, working at the front desk of the library. These walks were ever so slightly outside the confines of both of their lives and plans, outside the maps they had made, like those medieval maps that say "There be dragons"—the walks were on the edge of the dragon lands.

While Father Joe could no longer remember what justifications he had made for them, he could remember the steps they took, the place where the sidewalk became a dirt path, and then the dirt path ended by the willows along the river. He remembered how much he liked the way her hair surrounded her woolen cap and the way she walked with her arms tightly crossed against her woolen coat. Just once he had taken his gloved hand and brushed her hair out of her face in the wind. They had both been shocked by the gesture and had turned heads down and started walking toward campus again. But the memory of the gesture had remained, and he had returned to it many times. Sometimes he felt that it was nothing, a meaningless and instinctive moment. And other times, he felt it was everything, signaling a reach toward an entirely other world, a life he had wanted and not claimed, a vein of ore made through rock.

Had he thought of leaving the priesthood then? Had he thought of marrying her? Her letter suggested that this was something that had been available to him, that there had been such a choice and he had failed to make it. But "thought" was too strong a word. He couldn't say that he'd thought of it. Now he saw that it was there in all the natural warmth and honesty of her. She'd wanted to hear about his studies, wanted him to talk about himself, his professors, his own interests with a hunger that surprised him. He hadn't thought women were interested in such things.

But everything about her had been a surprise. Her fierce intelligence, her willingness to walk outside the lines with him, her anger about what she saw as her choices. "What choices?" she had said to him. "I can choose to be a nurse or a teacher. I don't like medicine, so I will be a teacher. I will get married and have as many children as possible and make sure they all learn their catechism."

And he was surprised when, in the spring, a few weeks before his birthday, she finally called it off.

"We can't keep doing this," she'd said. They were again by the river, but this time everything was pale green, as if a blanket had fallen across the land. The willows still held their buds tightly, but they spoke green nonetheless, and Joe had realized that he was looking forward to walking here with her through each season of the year, naming the changes as they saw them.

"Doing what?"

"This. Whatever it is we're doing. It isn't helping. We both have to do what we're called to do. Our duties."

Joe knew that if it had been up to him, he would've kept walking with her forever. He was a person of a basic inertia, and he had not minded the life lived on double tracks. But when she called it off, it was over. From then on there had only been one track, but apparently, some part of her had stayed there, paused inside of him, waiting by the other track, and her letter could bring back every speck of what he felt then, only sharper and clearer.

He returned the letter to its envelope and fingered the edge made by the letter opener. He raised the envelope to his nose and took a deep inhale. He smelled a faint hint of eucalyptus and maybe coffee, a hint of a domesticity far from him and his ordinary life. How strange to find yourself arrested in exactly the place where you left off, as if no time at all had passed, as if you were twenty-five again and yet also able to see that person, the young man, for the first time. He opened the center drawer of his desk and placed the letter and the letter opener inside.

From the bookshelf next to the desk, he drew a Hebrew lexicon, the Jerusalem Bible, a Hebrew Bible, and Klein's *A Comprehensive Etymological Dictionary of the Hebrew Language.* He had always been drawn to the most ancient language of the psalms, even though he had been trained to memorize them in Latin and he used them in English, especially the Jerusalem Bible whenever he prayed at a bedside or presided at a funeral. It was the Hebrew he craved, its earthy tones, its possibilities hidden inside letters that stood on the page like little houses. He opened his books to pages he had previously marked and pulled a yellow legal pad with a clean sheet forward. Psalm 49:4: "I turn my attention to a proverb, and set my solution to the harp," the Jerusalem Bible translation read. On the legal pad, he drew a chart, making long, unsteady lines down the page with a felt tip pen. At the top of one column, he wrote "to turn [my] attention"; at the top of another, he wrote "proverb"; at the top of the third, he wrote "solution." Under each of these, he put the Hebrew word responsible for that translation.

This was what he did sometimes in the afternoons. The yellow legal pad. The felt tip pen. The psalms, each verse a unique puzzle almost like a crossword or a word find, took him away when he perhaps should have been busy with parish life, visiting someone or drinking coffee at Willie's or refining his homily or changing the light bulbs in the entryway. Instead he stared at Hebrew letters as if they were runes and tried to see what other translators had not seen. He had several translations that he could take down from his shelf and add their attempts to his columns. The work reminded him of his days in seminary when he had hours to give to this, people to talk to about it. New insights arriving daily. Worlds opening in texts.

He felt this verse, as the Jerusalem Bible had it, was definitely missing something. The verse acted as though it were a problem/solution, and the words were all rather ugly compared to richer possibilities. There were many more open spaces than that translation allowed. For example, what the Jerusalem Bible had as "proverb" could be "parable" or simply "word," and "solution" was definitely wrong. It was something far less settled in the Hebrew, more like "enigma" or "mystery" or "the inexpressible." The poet is attempting to put into music something that can't be said, let alone solved. That seemed truer to Father Joe. The more you listened, the less you could make sense of things and yet the demand to express them grew. Under the columns, Joe experimented with possibilities. "I attend to the word and give music to the enigma." "I listen to the parable; its puzzle I play on the harp." "I listen as You speak, but my heart can only sing the inexpressible."

Father Joe loved Klein. What a beautiful man. He understood that translating Hebrew into English meant making a series of nearly invisible connections, of working from mystery toward something sometimes tawdry and too tidy and then working backward toward the mystery again. Klein's volume had cost him two hundred and thirty-five dollars, and he'd had to order it directly from the publisher. But living so far from a library, it was the only choice, and it had been worth it for the thin but somehow creamy pages and the careful attention to detail. He wanted to be the man who had written it.

But now into the mystery of the translation came Veronica. She was a person, Joe kept saying to himself. A real person. Not a memory. Not a figment of his imagination. In his imagination, she had been more of a color than a person: brown and gold. Why was that? Why those colors? Maybe they had been the colors of her hat and winter coat. She had lived a whole life without him, and yet she wrote as if they had never stopped talking. He tried to imagine what he might say in return. What tone might he take? What should he say about his life to date?

He hadn't realized that he was looking out the window toward the creek watching it run in spring ferment. Now the sun was dancing on the water, and he saw how far the spring had progressed. There was a dense green around the banks, and the creek was carrying snowmelt swiftly toward the Missouri. The letter had created some heat, he realized, in his cheeks, as if he were embarrassed about something.

He liked to remember that Veronica had spoken and that was the end of it. One track had disappeared. They'd both moved on. They'd left an imprint on each other, maybe, but little else. This meant that he was free to make her up, to imagine her. Whenever he did, he felt somehow chaste, even if that feeling was mixed up with longing. They had been so innocent, so delicate with each other.

But there had been other scenes, scenes he was loath to remember, scenes she was referring to in her letter. He'd waited for her outside her class. He'd come to the library when she was working and lurked nearby. "Lurked"—that was the word for it. He'd wanted one more conversation, one more walk. He'd wanted what they'd had, but he'd wanted it without consequence. "Didn't she like him? Didn't she enjoy their conversations?" "Couldn't they just . . ." He liked to remember that he had seen the truth of what she was saying right away and had accepted it, but no, that wasn't true.

She'd had to address him one more time.

She'd agreed to meet outside the library, and Joe had imagined they might walk down to the river in the full spring. He wanted what he wanted, and he'd imagined that she was giving in to him. But she'd stopped him as he'd turned on their familiar path.

"I'm getting married," she'd said. "I won't be back here next year."

"To whom?"

"It doesn't matter."

"It's someone your mother has chosen, isn't it?"

"So what if it is? What difference does it make to you?"

"Veronica, I . . ."

"You what?" She'd turned to him with that familiar ferocity that now had accusation in it. She waited a moment. He watched her anger blaze, turn curious, then subside.

"Goodbye, Joseph," she'd said, and walked away. There was your true end: the future Father Joe, standing speechless and choiceless on the sidewalk with the greening grass and the carefully trimmed hedges, the lilacs about to bloom. That remembrance, standing at the edge of the familiar longing, made his last cup of coffee turn slightly acid in his stomach.

The phone rang. He picked up the receiver automatically and held it against his ear. "St. Rose. Father Joseph speaking." He felt the receiver's weight like relief.

"Father Joe." He recognized Alice's voice. "Something has happened. It's Albert. Please come as soon as you can."

3

Where We Belong

HE WALKED QUICKLY up to the rectory and went inside to retrieve the Buick's keys. Lydia was there, preparing his supper in that robust way she had of taking over the whole house with her large energy. He poked his head into the kitchen and said, "Parish emergency," as if that were an excuse for him to say nothing more.

He drove the Buick along the creek, downstream toward Alice's house, the car maneuvering spring ruts and puddles from rain the day before. Albert was the oldest of Alice's children, and last Father Joe remembered, he was living in Rapid City, working construction. Father Joe tried to think through the details. Could he have gotten injured on the job? Would Alice need to get to Rapid City? Albert, he remembered, was a clever and big-hearted kid. He hid all of that behind a smart-ass exterior. You always wondered what he was making fun of you for, but at the same time, you could feel his affection. He had affection for his little brothers and sisters, for his mom, whom he never stopped teasing. Even for Father Joe. Pretty early in his adolescence, he'd decided to call Father Joe "Father-of-what." It wasn't a question. It was a statement. "Father-of-what!" he'd say when Father Joe pulled up in the Buick. And then he'd say, "wakalapi?"

the Lakota word for coffee, as if he were being polite, but his eyes flickered to let you know the joke was still on. He knew Father Joe liked his mom's coffee.

When Father Joe pulled up in front of the house, the sun had dropped behind the cottonwoods and cast a soft light over the weedy ground. Bear was sitting on the front step. At thirteen, he had decided to grow his dark, wavy hair long over the front of his face, and he brushed it back with a practiced motion of his hand when he saw Father Joe's car. Unlike Albert, whose thoughts and feelings played constantly over his face, Bear never showed much emotion. His green eyes watched everything, everyone, and recorded what they saw in a sketchbook that he kept with him almost always. Father Joe tried to think of the last time he'd seen Bear without a sketchbook. He had it now, of course, open on his lap. But he didn't seem intent on anything.

"Bear," Father Joe said. "Your mother called me."

The boy nodded. "She's inside," he said. "On the phone."

Father Joe sat beside Bear on the step. Bear moved over slightly.

"You okay?" Father Joe asked.

"It's not me. It's Albert."

"I know, but still. I wanted to check." Father Joe waited. Bear turned back to his sketchbook as if to indicate the end of the conversation.

Father Joe stood and wiped the dust off the back of his pants. He opened the screen door and squinted in the dim light. Alice was standing between the tiny living room and even tinier kitchen where there was a phone attached to the wall. She had the phone against her ear. "Can I leave my number?" she was saying into it slowly, like the person on the other end might be having a hard time understanding her. "Thank you," she said finally, and hung up.

She sank down into the plastic seat of a worn chair at the table and looked at him. "I don't know if I can . . ." she said, and then her voice trailed off.

It was a bit like an out-of-body experience, the way that Father Joe reached over and put his hand on her head, her hair stiff and thick under his hand, and then offered her a blessing. He meant it in a way that might give her some kind of strength, might fill her. But his hand acted separately from head and heart, as if he had been shifted out of alignment and broken into three pieces. This was his job. To show up. To make an offering. She'd asked him to come, after all. Some inner argument broke out inside Father Joe, a defensive voice telling him he was right where he belonged and another voice challenging his very presence.

He sat down at the table, and they looked at each other. He tried to read her eyes: angry, frightened, sick, but also searching for something that she was likely to find only deep inside herself. He wondered if he could ask what happened.

"There was a fight, apparently," she said finally, as if she doubted every word of it. "Some bar in Rapid. And Albert." She shifted in the chair, then stood and walked over to the wall in the kitchen, leaned against it, and put her hand over her mouth, as if preventing herself from speaking the next set of words.

"They said he was beaten. Bad."

"Hospital?"

"He's in the hospital. He hasn't woken up. They said they could tell me more in a couple of hours."

By the time the hospital called, the house had already begun to fill with people. One woman—Father Joe tried to trace the relation. Was it Alice's cousin? Or half sister? Or?—had brought a chicken half-cooked in a pot and set it on the stove. Another woman was rolling out fry bread at the table. Several men Father Joe didn't know, but dimly recognized, had taken up residence on the porch. Three of Father Joe's parishioners, two women and a man who were regulars like Alice, had heard the news and come as well. They were sitting in the living room, and Father Joe went and greeted each of them and then stood helplessly between the living room and the kitchen.

Bear came in, took a look around, and went out again. Father Joe followed him. "Hey, do you want to walk down to the creek?" he asked. Bear shrugged.

They were halfway down the path when they heard the wailing. It was like a sound coming not from the house, but like the world had been torn and the cry came from out of the other place. Neither of them had ever heard Alice make that sound. They both turned, without speaking, and ran back up the path toward the house.

———

Albert's casket arrived from Rapid City in the back of a pickup truck. "Didn't the funeral home have any hearses?" Father Joe asked the driver.

"Yeah," the driver said, and looked Father Joe over, taking in collar and shined shoes. The young man had deep pockmarks in his cheeks. He reddened a little as he said, "They said they wouldn't bring one out here in the spring."

He and several other young men jumped onto the bed of the truck and unloaded the casket, which they carried into the living room. Alice's sister hung a star quilt behind it. Albert's father had come up from Rapid and was wandering around the house in a cowboy hat like a lost child. Father Joe looked at him and felt some affinity. Who ever knew what to do in these situations?

Father Joe himself, who was supposed to know, stood by the door, then in the kitchen where Alice's oldest daughter, Marlena, was directing traffic, and the women were loading the table with potatoes and Crock-Pots of soup and packages of cookies and bags of Cheetos. He envied them for a moment because their work seemed so necessary and straightforward. He worried that it might look like he wanted to eat and someone would offer him a plate. He'd be the first one eating. That would be embarrassing. So he went out to stand on the porch while people arranged things inside. He came in when he saw other people with mugs of coffee. He went over to the percolator and poured some into a Styrofoam cup. "Sugar, Father?" One of the women asked. Rosalinda? That was her name. He was almost sure of it.

Lydia had come in and bustled around with her intense energy and her easy belonging. She knew everyone's names. She asked about their relatives. She set down her macaroni and cheese with pride of place. He watched her and wondered what the others made of her. Father Joe always felt a little scolded by her, but then scolding was her way of saying, "I accept you. You are one of mine." So Father Joe didn't mind it, necessarily.

Alice had taken a chair next to the casket and sat there accepting people's greetings with quiet dignity. Someone had put a shawl around her shoulders. Father Joe looked at her from across the room. He tried not to stare, but he noticed how grief had deepened the lines in her face, and he thought, inadvertently, *We are growing old together.* Then he chided himself for that imagined intimacy. They were not growing old together. They were growing old, and life was doing what life does, which is piling loss onto loss.

The evening light lingered long across the lot. Father Joe went outside as the sun was setting, in gold and green, and looked toward the creek, where the vegetation thickened and dark came sooner. He saw a shadow of Bear there. It looked like he was there with other boys. Father Joe recognized him by that familiar gesture of his hand across his face to momentarily move the hair to the side, one hand deep in a pocket.

After dark, Father Joe went up to the casket and laid a hand on Albert's forehead. He made the sign of the cross and then made it again across Albert's chest. He put a small statue of St. Christopher, the patron saint of travelers, into the casket. He couldn't hear Albert's ringing voice in his head. He couldn't feel the laughter of him. Everything he might be able to feel was trapped in the shadows around the casket.

He laid a hand on Alice's shoulder. She had not moved in several hours. Someone had brought a paper plate of food, and it sat beside her untouched. She nodded.

"You're always welcome here, Father," she said in a quiet voice, as if in some kind of trance.

The words had a strange effect on Father Joe. All the days he had spent in exactly this place. If he wasn't welcome here, where was he welcome? And why had Alice spoken those strange words? Where had they come from? Had someone suggested he wasn't welcome? And now, a panic set in as he fumbled through his options. Did she mean he had overstayed his welcome and he should go?

He couldn't ask her what she meant. There was no place in the tightness of grief for that. But his awkwardness appeared more obvious than ever. He stood in his collar, in his shiny shoes and his pressed slacks, amid all of these people so easy in their skin, so sure of who they were as he imagined it. Set apart, separated, to fill a function. Was he the only person in that room who was more function than person?

Just then the drums started outside, where someone had built a fire. The smell of the smoke started to drift into the living room, and when the tears did come to Father Joe's eyes, he recognized the self-pity in them, and he quickly wiped them away.

Near midnight, Father Joe went outside again and stood on the porch, looking out toward the road. The wind had died down. The cottonwoods were quiet. The young men who had started the drumming and had now stopped were standing around the bonfire they had made. Lights from their cigarettes flickered through the shadows. Father Joe recognized a few of them, kids who had grown up with Albert, but there were others he didn't know at all. One of them was dressed in a red bandana and a leather jacket with motorcycle-riding pants, like he'd come from the Sturgis Motorcycle Rally. There was something in the way he stood that Father Joe instinctively didn't like. He immediately named it cockiness, arrogance, but the man stirred the air around him and drew attention to himself. Father Joe felt a desire to stand between him and the house, as if he shouldn't come in.

Alice's daughter, Jackie, came up beside Father Joe and stood for a moment. She was almost eighteen, the youngest of the kids before Bear had arrived. She reminded him of Alice in some ways. She had a quick wit and sharp eyes, but she was also more delicate, a little lighter on her feet, almost like a fairy child.

"That one there," she said to Father Joe, indicating the man in the bandana. "He was with Albert when he got in that fight. He's probably the only one who knows what happened. Vincent." She tried out his name in her mouth. "Vincent," she said again, almost as if to call him but not loud enough that he could hear. At that moment, Vincent looked up and directly at them standing on the porch. Jackie disappeared into the house, and Father Joe kept looking toward Vincent and the fire and the other young men with an uneasy feeling.

Father Joe was refilling his coffee in the kitchen when Bear finally went and stood beside the casket. Where had he been all of these hours, Joe wondered. He came a little closer as he watched the boy approach the casket and stand, staring down at his brother's face. Bear was slight compared to other boys his age. He looked younger than he was as he stood there and made a fist, like he was getting ready to punch his brother in the face.

"You are stupid to be dead," he said. Then he covered his face with his hands and went to sit on the floor next to Alice with his knees up to his chest. Jackie knelt down next to him and put her arms around him.

The funeral mass was the next day. The church was filled to over-flowing. The star quilt that had hung behind Albert all night now draped over his coffin. Father Joe at last knew what to do. All his moves were scripted. He knew where to stand and what to say and how to say it. He tried to convey Albert's sense of humor, his contagious laughter, his bighearted love for his family. He tried to say something about Christian hope, about the triumph of life over death. As he mulled it over later, he wasn't sure how well it had come out or if it was, after all, a comfort to Alice.

Afterward Father Joe saw Bear by the edge of the church, not far from the place where his cardboard box had been found. The lilac bush by the door was now in full bloom and the smell of it made Father Joe's nose itch. He went over to the boy and stood.

"You doing okay?"

He nodded and kicked at the mud with his sneaker. Father Joe cleared his throat and searched for another question to ask, but Bear spoke first.

"Why'd they kill him?"

"I don't think they know who did it yet. The police said they don't know."

"Vincent knows. He says it was the wasichu. He says that even though he was there, the police haven't even interviewed him yet. He says there's not even going to be an investigation because they don't care if some Indian guy dies on the street."

"We don't know what happened. Vincent says he knows a lot of things, but I am not sure he does, to be honest." Father Joe squinted toward the west, where cumulus clouds were forming. Even the word "Vincent" carried something sinister toward them, introducing something in their midst that Father Joe didn't like. Or maybe it was that word *wasichu.* He tried to shift the subject away from Vincent.

"Anyway, it's important to remember that we all make choices, and Albert's choice to be on that street, at that bar, to get into a fight—those were mistakes. That's a bad situation to put your-self in."

"I thought you said that we didn't know what happened."

"We don't. That's true. It's just people sometimes put them-selves in situations where bad things are more likely to happen."

Father Joe's chest constricted as he felt the words fall empty between them, like drops of sweat into the mud. He was trying to say something protective, something Bear might mull over that might be good for him. But he could feel the failure, how he had only increased the distance between them.

Bear shrugged and tossed the hair from his eyes. He stared down at the patchy grass. Father Joe thought of something that Alice said about the word *wasichu.* It wasn't a color—even though a lot of people, like Vincent, used it to mean white—it was a dis-eased state of mind. *Those who steal the fat of the land.* Every time Father Joe heard the word, he pictured his grandparents' ranch, the way it stretched to the horizon, with a smattering of buildings here and there. He thought about the way he and his brothers played under the few trees, cowboys and Indians. Later they spent whole summers building the fence line, repairing the fence line, hours and hours spent pounding fence posts into the ground, fixing wire. Ours; not ours. Each fence post a ritual statement. Our land, our cows, our family.

If the world was divided into wasichu and Lakota (and Lakota meant "friend"), then who was Father Joe—on which side of the fence posts now?

And what about Bear? Where had he come from? Where were his people? Was there a woman watching him grow into a man from a distance? Was that woman wasichu or Lakota? Until now, no one around Bear had cared about that question—it hardly ever came up, but now it hovered. Where would Bear belong?

4

Animated Clay

SINCE ALBERT'S DEATH, Veronica's letter had stayed in the drawer, next to the letter opener. Whenever he walked into his office, he felt it, like an energy, an aura, a vibration. *I wonder. I wonder about you.*

He had started to write back in his mind. *I have often heard your voice calling my name.* But then, in his mind, he erased that. It felt too romanticized. What was he trying to do here anyway? Revive a friendship? Start an affair? Be polite? It felt silly, like someone else's life.

He tried: *Sometimes I make a map in my mind of that other life, the one I lived with you.* He liked that. It felt both abstract and personal. And it was true. In the broadest of outlines, he had sketched that other life, although he had never really gotten specific about it. It was more of a feeling. *I imagine it would have been a warmer life. Here I am so exposed to the wind.*

That was certainly not the letter he was going to write. He enjoyed the game in his mind of trying to match her tone of bravery and honesty, of trying to say what was true but also toe the line that kept him safe.

In his office, he sat down once again with his lexicon and his psalms. He tried to enter Klein's world, where language was substance and Hebrew letters were like little bodies. It was like they sometimes walked off the page and arranged themselves on his desk. I should have been a professor, he thought. He imagined an office in a university, preferably on an upper floor where he could look down on a green quad. He imagined students, with that inquisitive openheartedness that Veronica had had and his own, somewhat self-absorbed, exuberance.

That door had closed with a lot of other doors, during those first years after seminary, when things with Father Rossling had gone so badly. He could almost hear the doors slamming in his head.

Albert's death had been so absorbing that Father Joe was still on Psalm 49. The real puzzle in this psalm was the Hebrew word *nephesh*. English translators kept it pretty simple. They went for "life," typically, and maybe he was making things more complicated than they needed to be. That would be like him. But the word went so much deeper than that. Nephesh was composed of three little bodies: nun, peh, shin. Each letter was not only a particular shape, it was also a kind of resonance, and each letter had a great deal associated with it. Images, regions of the human body, particular energies. When these were placed side by side in something we call a word, they didn't so much make meaning as breathe into it, enliven it. And of all words, nephesh had this mysterious quality in abundance.

In this psalm, the nephesh is "ransomed" by God. God saves the nephesh, when the clutches of death reach out and threaten to overcome it. Some translators drew nephesh close to the Greek psyche, a quality of mind, cognition as well as an animating force inside the person. This led toward another common translation: soul. But this was really too abstract for Hebrew, which tended to keep its feet pretty well on the ground. "Soul" hinted at some kind of afterlife and psyche at some mind separate from a body. When a nephesh was "ransomed," it definitely had Christian connotations of payment for the now disembodied soul at death. That was what many Catholic translators were going for anyway. But nephesh isn't about life after death. Nephesh is the life force breathed into Adam by God at creation. So could you simply translate it as breath? *God ransoms the breath.* That is nice because of the connection to singing, to the harp. But how does God save breath?

Nephesh was animated clay combined with some kind of mind—blood and breath and something more. Father Joe liked the play of "God saves the animated clay," although it was really hard to know what that meant. But these translations were ultimately for him, after all. It was between him and the legal pad. It was his own searching for the place where heaven and earth crossed, a place that was sometimes so much easier to find in Hebrew than in English. Maybe he could write to Veronica about this work. Maybe she would understand it and could even help him try to make sense of it.

———

He looked up from his desk and out the window. He was surprised to see Bear walking down the slope from the church toward the cottonwood-studded creek, now in full summer swell. He looked to see if Bear had a fishing pole. He did not. He was walking purposefully toward the path that ran along the water.

A little while later—verse nine—Father Joe stood and stretched. He checked his watch. Lydia would have dinner on the table at the rectory precisely at six. He had half an hour or so—maybe he'd walk himself down to the creek path, stretch his legs, get some fresh air. The angle of the sun was soft through the trees and the water sparkled. He wondered if Bear was still down that way. He could have walked all the way home from there.

Instinctively, Father Joe turned left instead of right when he reached the path. Right led downstream, toward Alice's house, and left led upstream and ended eventually in the bluffs behind the church. He walked a little stiffly at first, working the blood back down into his joints, feeling the effects of the day, the long study, the uninterrupted hours that he had not had for some time.

Up ahead he saw a figure, and soon he knew that figure was Bear. He was walking toward Father Joe with his hands buried deep in the pockets of his jeans. Father Joe then saw him pull one hand out to wipe his sleeve across his face then bury the hand in his pocket again.

At closer range, even in the dimming light, Father Joe could see a dark shadow around Bear's eye.

"What happened?"

Bear looked away.

"What's going on? Where have you been?"

"I hate him."

"Hate who?" Even as he said the word, he knew the answer. Vincent.

"He's stupid."

"Did he hit you?"

"He said my daddy was a white trash honkey from Pierre."

"Bear, you can't go around . . ." Father Joe raised a hand to his forehead and rubbed it. "You need to cool it, buddy."

Bear swung his hair out of his eyes for a moment and looked at Father Joe, squinting, a glance, and then he quickly looked down again, but Father Joe had seen the bruise blooming into a multitude of colors.

In a moment, Bear was gone down the path toward home, running, leaving a soft shadow of dust rising behind him, and Father Joe was left standing with the evening falling around him. From somewhere, a pipit sang a mating song. There was no way to recover what he had just lost.

Maybe it was good, Father Joe thought as he turned toward the rectory. Maybe this would put an end to the Vincent fascination that had risen up around Alice's whole family. They had this idea, Alice included, that Vincent knew something about

Albert's death, something he didn't trust them enough to tell them and that if they could draw him closer, the truth would be revealed. Their grief had gotten mixed up with this fixation on a man, a fixation that filled Father Joe with unease.

Vincent had hung around. Didn't he have somewhere to be? Father Joe thought impatiently. A job back in Rapid? A girlfriend somewhere? But no, he had stayed on Windy Creek, day in and day out, a fixture on Alice's porch. Father Joe had often heard his motorcycle from his office window, if it was open, speeding toward Willie's. Sometimes Jackie was on the back of it. At first Father Joe thought he was a freeloader, nothing more than that, but gradually it was becoming clear that he had bigger plans. He was courting Jackie.

Bear too watched the man with some confused combination of fascination and hatred. Alice had told Father Joe about a particularly worrisome incident in which Vincent had taken Bear aside and showed him his knife, with an intricate silver and pearl inlay. "You can't never be too careful," he'd told Bear. "Someone might come up behind you. You gotta be ready." He'd let Bear hold the knife and practice snapping it in and out of the handle.

"I don't like him," Father Joe had said to Alice. "He's bad news." She had been standing in front of the altar at St. Rose dusting while Father Joe sat in the front pew. The afternoon was quiet. A bright June sun came through the stained glass, making patterns across the worn carpet like skin with bright wounds.

She had sighed. Albert's death had taken a toll on her. She seemed dulled by it, fogged. Her eyes had a smokier color in them. Father Joe sometimes felt like he was talking through cotton in her direction.

"I know, Father." She shook her head. "You know what he calls Bear? Iyeska. Mixed blood." She looked toward Father Joe. "I told him, you know what, misun, mixed is a state of mind."

So maybe Bear's black eye, his report of the incident, would be enough. Alice would tell Vincent to go, Jackie would see him for what he was, and whatever secret he was keeping about Albert's death would go back with him to wherever he came from. Good riddance.

By the time Father Joe arrived back at the rectory, Lydia had gone. She'd left the light on in the kitchen and his meatloaf on a plate on the kitchen table covered by a towel. Joe took a tumbler and the whiskey out of the cupboard and added ice to the bottom. He poured two fingers full. He looked at the phone for a minute and wondered about calling Alice to see if Bear had gotten home okay, and if he'd accurately reported what had happened. He wanted to hear in her voice that sharp cadence of knowing, that definitive tone he had relied on. That Vincent's days were numbered.

On the other hand, he now heard the same voice in his head that he had heard at the wake, when he had suddenly stepped out of his skin and seen himself standing there with them all, one of them and not one of them. Ridiculous, the voice now said. Ridiculous. He thought of what he'd said to Bear, "Cool it." He saw himself for a moment through the boy's eyes and felt a streak of contrition all the way through him like a kind of slow-moving lightning bolt. The boy seemed too hot all the time, too angry. His anger had become the number one thing that Father Joe ran into when he saw him, like a blast of heat. Father Joe saw that he wanted something of the old Bear back, that creative, quiet boy with the watching eyes. The Bear of the Sketchbook, always sketching, always taking in. Since Albert died, he had been replaced by this other creature, one who would challenge a grown man to a fight by the creek. A grown man with a knife? What in the world did Bear think he was going to get out of that exchange? But Father Joe saw that he could have met him better. Maybe he could have waited and asked a question, maybe Bear would have gentled and told him something. Instead, he'd chased him off. Ridiculous.

The meatloaf was a bit cold; the green beans had a gleam of gelatinous margarine. Lydia was trying to take care of his heart by cutting down on the butter.

While he ate, he pulled the pad of paper they kept by the phone toward him and took a pen from the front pocket of his shirt.

Dear Veronica,

I am so sorry for how long it has taken me to write to you. Your letter arrived in the midst of a crisis here with one of our families and I've only now had the opportunity to sit down and write.

———

No. That wasn't it. She would know the tone immediately as fear. He had to write back—that part was an obligation. But everything else, everything beyond the mere fact of writing, was on the same side of transgression as their walks down to the river had been. Now he understood that it was his impossible job to find the path between obligation and transgression. He felt angry with her for a moment, for putting him in such an awkward position.

He tore the sheet from the pad. It took a little glue with it as it went. He drank the whiskey quickly, feeling the familiar burn rise and subside, then he tried again.

Dear Veronica,

I have by now memorized your letter and begun so many letters to you in my head, I hardly know where to begin.

I was delighted to hear from you. There was a way in which you had become more of a story to me than a person. It was a story I

told to myself about my own life. "Once, on my way to becoming
a priest, I met a woman. And I almost didn't become a priest. But
then I did."

Now I understand that you have lived for years and years
beyond me, have had another life. You are not my story to tell.

———

He got up from the table and walked toward the sink with his
plate. He placed it inside, then set the tea kettle on the stove,
each gesture a familiar ritual. He'd left the back door open, and
moths now had begun to throw themselves at the screen like
tiny penitents, intent on self-flagellation.

My own story is not easy to tell. I feel like I've stumbled here
by accident and then stayed a long time. There are so many
ways I could tell you this story. I am here as an exile, partly
self-imposed, partly imposed by those who wanted to be rid of
me. I am here on a mission to a beautiful, abandoned people who
deserve better than they've gotten. I am here because, after some
decisions came down from above, I did what they told me. I am
here because God sent me.

Which version of me would you like, Veronica? I can offer you
the dedicated parish priest, going through the motions in a tough
place as best he can, or the exiled, jaded radical who couldn't
fight back and has been lost ever since.

Each one of these versions has its pros and cons. Lately,
I admit, it has all seemed a little more con than pro.

———

This was not the kind of letter likely to have an end. Already
he felt like he'd opened a wound, and it would now bleed out
onto the page. Maybe the nephesh was not in the blood or in
the breath or in the clay, maybe it was in the ink. God save his
nephesh, then. Ransom him from the pit of his own making.

The next day, Father Joe drove to the post office after mass. He decided to mail the letter using the box on the outside of the post office. He'd spent an inordinate amount of time on this, lying on his bed in the dark, going through the options in his head. Where to mail the letter. How to mail the letter. It had been tempting to drive all the way to Hanson and post the letter from there. He didn't need anyone on Windy Creek to notice that he was writing to a woman. He tried to picture Jolene, at the counter inside the post office, looking at him for a moment too long as he cheerfully pushed the letter toward her, her eyes lighting up with the possibility of gossip but her lips staying in a straight line. It was a dull job—the post office on Windy Creek. Sometimes you had to invent your fun. He'd really rather not be on that side of things. Wasn't it Jerome Trudeau who worked in the back and got the mail onto the truck? He came to mass on Sundays sometimes with his elderly mother. Did that make him more trustworthy or less trustworthy? Did he pay attention to the mail as he sorted it?

He'd popped it into the blue box by the side of the post office anyway with a little extra postage, just in case. The last thing he wanted was some kind of "return to sender" mark on it. The bravest thing he'd done in years, perhaps, and not exactly brave.

5

Ordinary Time

ON A SUNDAY IN JULY, Father Joe walked down from the rectory in the early sun. He was thinking about his homily. The text was from Luke's gospel: "The apostles said to Jesus: Increase our faith." Jesus's response was not particularly encouraging: "If you had faith even the size of a mustard seed, you'd be able to say to this tree, 'Be uprooted and plant yourself in the sea' and it would obey you." The implication of which, he thought, was that the apostles did not, in fact, have faith even the size of a mustard seed. They were asking for an increase from nothing.

And the next part also wasn't giving Father Joe a lot of easy fodder either. In the second part Jesus tells them that even when the servant comes in from the field, he still keeps working. Do you even say thank you to the servant? Jesus asks. No. The servant is only doing what he was told to do. Don't expect gratitude, the passage seems to say. And don't expect faith. Just do your job.

What was Father Joe supposed to say to his little flock about this? That they didn't work hard enough? That they didn't have the faith of a mustard seed? Maybe he would say, "You can take that little bit of faith that you've got and you can really do something with it." But that felt falsely encouraging. Maybe it was:

in the kingdom of heaven, things that look small are actually great. Look around. What are the smallest things you know? For Jesus the smallest thing he knew was a mustard seed. How is that small thing great in the kingdom of heaven?

He looked out over the road. The reservation baked in July. It felt almost apocalyptic how the land became bereft of water, how the ground crackled under his shoes. Rain, you wanted to beg to the sky, rain.

The good thing about a homily, anyway, was how short it was. You really only had to say one nice thing and call it good. "The homily is a moment of light in the darkness," his homiletics professor had said once—a sweet, old man with a saggy face who was giving way to scoliosis.

That's what the people wanted anyway when the sun was rising and starting to beat against the west wall of the church. You had to keep it short. He could see the paint peeling even from his distance of a hundred feet. It took a pounding: relentless sun in the summer, wind in those brief weeks standing in for spring and fall, and then snow and wind all winter long. The heart could feel like this, couldn't it? Battered? Peeling?

But he wasn't going to get it painted this summer. The first thing to think about was the roof. Water damage was seeping out along both east and west walls. Maybe if Father Joe had faith the size of a mustard seed, he could say "Roof—be fixed!" and it would be fixed. Maybe he could joke about that during the sermon and then people could get the idea that the roof was not going to fix itself. But he didn't like to have those kinds of subtle messages attached to sermons. That had been one of Rossling's favorite tricks. Mix in a little bit of scripture with a little bit of scolding. Call it motivation.

When Father Joe opened the creaky door to the church, everything inside was still quiet. He was the first to arrive. The threshold was one of his favorite places, a place where you could still feel the relationship between in and out. Outside wind. Inside buffer. Outside the restless, endless sea of prairie. Inside shelter. It was a pause, a space that opened between worlds. A moment and then gone.

Alice usually came to Saturday night mass and then stayed after to make sure everything was ready for Sunday. His vestments were pressed and in the cupboard—black robe with a green stole for ordinary time. The paten and chalice were laid out. The lectionary was properly marked with its ribbon. Silence fell over everything in readiness.

When Father Joe walked out of the sacristy at nine, he surveyed the room. The usual suspects. Mary and Wallace. Frank. Bonnie. Dennis and his mother. Jerome and his mother. Saturday night generally brought more people out, so the Sunday mass was smaller, but Father Joe had yet to reckon with the fact that the Church of the Apostles of the Resurrected Savior, which had started meeting in an abandoned warehouse on Highway 15, had started to draw more and more people away from mass. People liked the singing, they said. They liked the energy.

But there was one woman he didn't recognize. She sat three pews from the back on the aisle, as if she might want to make a quick escape. As Father Joe raised his hands and said, "May God be with you," the thought came to him suddenly and sent a sharp pain from his throat directly to his bladder. Veronica. She had a mass of white and brown curls pulled back from her face and piled up randomly but elegantly on her head. She wore a plain khaki dress with short sleeves and a belt. He felt like there was a kind of soft light emanating from her. Maybe that wasn't her. And then, *Oh, no. It's her.*

The rest of the mass was a blur. He raised his hands as if they belonged to someone else. He spoke words but hardly recognized his own voice, and when he did he cringed inwardly. How must all of this sound to her? He listened to the western wind, picking up now, shake the walls of the church, and he imagined it lifting up the little building and sending it across the prairie like tumbleweed, and he almost wished it would.

He got through it somehow—force of habit—even managing to place a wafer on her tongue with only a slight tremble, which she most likely noticed. "Amen," she said. He interrogated that voice. Was it the one he knew? Did he remember it? He'd smiled a little to indicate recognition but then felt like the muscles of his mouth had trapped themselves against the sides of his face and he couldn't release them.

After the benediction, he lingered in the sacristy, putting away his vestments with care, rinsing the chalice and paten. He wanted to give her time to escape if she wanted to, relieve them both of the burden of going forward from here. Now that she'd seen him, she might have seen enough.

But when he came out, she was standing on the gravel drive-way with a purse over one arm that she was holding across her body like the wind might blow it away. He could see in her both the young girl with her arms tightly folded across her woolen coat and the middle-aged lady, come from church.

"Hello," he said from a distance of several steps—too far almost to be heard in the wind. She shielded her eyes from the sun and dust and turned toward him. "Father," she smiled.

"Joseph," he said.

"Joseph, then," she nodded.

"You came a long way. I wish I had known. I would have . . ."

"It's nothing. I wanted to see you. See your 'tough place.'"

They paused in the wind. Father Joe rocked on his heels. It had been pretty bold of her to come. Would he have done the same?

"Would you like to have dinner with me? I was about to." He gestured toward the rectory. He knew that there would be a covered dish in the oven. Lydia only came once on Sundays, and she generally put a casserole there that he could eat for both the noon meal and later for supper. He'd also driven over to Hanson last week and laid in a fresh bottle of white wine, so that was there too.

They walked up the path. Father Joe found himself conscious of the exact space between them, how many steps. He was careful not to move in too close. As they approached the rectory, he suddenly felt how shabby it was, the door on its fragile hinges, a tear in the screen that he hadn't seen before. He'd have to ask Dennis to have a look at it next week. The entryway smelled of dust—and was it age? What might she see here? It could only be something to pity, he thought wildly, a life poorly inhabited.

Or maybe she saw that other possibility: faithfulness. No mansions on the hill here. No velvet slippers. Separateness but not decadence. She might appreciate that, after all. I guess, he thought, it was a bit hard to know what kind of a Catholic she had become. They were all over the map these days. He might ask.

Inside he extracted two wineglasses from the armoire and rinsed them in the sink. He wiped them with a towel and set them on the dining room table as if this were something he did every Sunday, while she stood in the doorway between the kitchen and the more formal dining room.

He'd expected, if he could have expected this meeting, to find her more familiar. He didn't recognize her voice, for example. If she had been in another room and started speaking, he wouldn't have known it was Veronica. Her voice was deeper and had more notes and resonances than the young woman's voice. But it still had that peculiar effect that it had had on him as a young man: that he was tuned in to hear it and had been listening for it.

They sat down in the paneled dining room, with its impersonal furniture, meant obviously for a more social priest than the one he had been. The covered dish was chicken in mushroom sauce. He poured the wine and proposed a toast, "To old friends." She lifted her glass.

"So this is Windy Creek." She looked around. "Home of the famous Father Joseph Kreitzer, priest to the Sioux."

"Famous, am I now? It's hard to say that without irony."

"People do like to romanticize."

He held his wineglass and watched the light catch the pale liquid. He began to tell her about an incident at the church the week before when the good people of Sacred Heart in Beaumont had called to say that they had some things to donate to the reservation's St. Vincent de Paul Society. He'd driven all the way there in the Buick only to discover that they had a truckload of stuff—cribs and strollers and furniture and several garbage bags of used clothing—all piled in their parking lot waiting for him to haul away. When they'd seen the expression on his face, they'd said, "Oh, didn't Shirley tell you to bring something bigger?" When he'd asked if maybe they might have a truck to bring it over in, the faces of the Catholic Daughters had frozen into an expression no one could call a smile. "We don't have anybody who could . . ." He'd filled in the blank on his own: drive to the reservation.

When he'd started the story, he'd meant it to be a mix of funny and realistic, something to cut through the Mother Teresa garbage that people sometimes cast over his life—that *Midwest Catholic Reporter* piece she'd mentioned reading Exhibit A. He'd wanted to find some clever ending and imagined them both laughing about it. But the ending turned bitter in his mouth. It was an indictment. And she'd heard it.

She shifted a little in her chair and brushed the curls away from her face. "I've long wanted to apologize for something."

The light in the room was mottled, going from bright to dark in quick succession as clouds moved across the sun. Joe had not switched the dining room lights on and now wondered if he should.

"Our last meeting. All of those years ago. The way I behaved. I was so sure of myself, so sure I was doing the right thing. There was so much righteous indignation from me, and I've needed to say I'm sorry." She was looking at him intently, as if she had practiced this speech and had very much wanted to see what effect it would have on him.

"I don't think there's any need for an apology," he said. His voice was softer than he'd meant it to be. "I couldn't see the position I was putting you in."

She echoed his softness. "I wanted to tell you. I don't know if it's right. But I wanted to tell you that I've very often dreamed about you. It's the strangest thing. Vivid, and there's usually this sense that we've crossed some kind of bridge together. We've gotten from one side to the other. But one time, this was years ago, I dreamed that you were in trouble and I reached out for you, but I couldn't find you." She shrugged. "I guess I needed you to know that."

Which part, he wondered, had she needed to say? That she had reached? Or that she couldn't find?

"I thought I might reach out to you, literally." She laughed. "After that. But I never did." She waved her hand in front of her face as if trying to chase something away.

He could feel the day deepening around them, and he thought of her trip back. She'd need to get on the road if she was going to get home before dark. It was a good four or five hours to Harrisburg. But he didn't want to say anything about it, like he was pushing her out the door or she'd overstayed her welcome. He wondered what conversations she'd had to have and with whom to drive all the way out here on a Sunday and what she'd said about going back. He tried, for a moment, to picture Darel on the other side of the state, waiting for his wife. Did Darel play golf on Sunday? Did he go to the club and have a drink?

This all felt like a game with no rules. The priesthood was a series of practiced gestures. When you boiled it down and you took out all the spiritualization, that's really what it was. Lift this, say this. Gestures. If a priest showed up and did nothing more than go through the motions, but did it adequately, you could say the man had done his job, even if he was hardly human in doing it. But here, with her, there were no prescribed gestures. He didn't know what to do. He felt tired. That fatigue always crept up and bit him on Sunday afternoons.

She felt the shift in his attention and stood up from the table.

"I'll write to you again."

"I'll welcome that."

"Let's be friends, can we?"

"Indeed." The word felt laden to him, like the heaviest word he'd ever said. Thirty years of the unspoken in it.

He walked her to the door, and when they stood for a moment in front of the screen, he grasped her hand and then lifted it to his lips. When he dropped it, he was surprised to see tears in her eyes. She turned away and walked down the path toward her car waiting in the dust below the sage-covered hill.

6

Ghost Lake

BEAR'S RUN-IN with Vincent had not had the effect Father Joe had hoped. It had been weeks since the incident and still, Vincent hung around, ubiquitous at Alice's house, ruining Father Joe's Sundays. In fact, things had only gotten worse. If Father Joe was to understand correctly, because no one had said it to him, Jackie and Vincent had gotten an apartment together on the other side of the bluffs where the government had recently built some cheap row houses. Vincent was with them to stay.

Late one night in August, his bedroom window open to catch any breeze, Father Joe heard tires on the gravel driveway outside. He had been sleeping lightly but was instantly awake with a sensation of panic overtaking him, that heart-clutching sensation that had started to worry him. An engine cut and then he heard several steps toward the front door. He was already getting dressed when Alice's voice came with the knocking.

He met her at the door, his collar in his pocket. She was wearing sweatpants and a tank top in the heat. He noticed the shape of her breasts against the ribbed fabric. Her hair was pulled back into a ponytail. Whatever had happened had pulled her from bed in an instant.

"Take your car," she said. He followed her out onto the highway, and they drove toward her house. The darkness on the highway, even with the lights from her car and from his, was darker on the reservation. There were no streetlights or shop windows lit up against the night. But the night sky was hazy, and there were few stars. No one felt the need to protect themselves against such darkness the way they did in the city.

At Alice's house lights blazed, and inside preparations were being made. Marlena was still barefoot, but she was packing what looked like knapsacks with sandwiches and Cokes in the kitchen. Alice's second son, Eli, who they called Rabbit for that quick, darting look on his face, was sketching something at the table.

"Where's Bear?" Father Joe said.

"That's the question," Alice said. Her old self had stepped out in what was apparently a crisis. She was clear and taut.

She laid out the facts, so far as she knew them.

Vincent had been stabbed, rushed to Rapid, and there was as yet no word on his condition. Jackie was unconscious and in the hospital. Alice was going there. Bear was missing. Father Joe and Rabbit were going to search for him. Rabbit was taking the east side. Father Joe was taking the west side. Marlena was going to stay at home and call the hospital if Bear appeared.

Rabbit handed Father Joe a roughly sketched map. Rabbit was taking Ghost Lake and east. Joe was taking everything west of Ghost Lake. Marlena handed him a knapsack and a flashlight. Alice had spoken and had gone.

Rabbit had already pulled out of the driveway in his rusted Dodge Dart when Father Joe got into his car and stared at his map. He drove to Ghost Lake and parked along the weedy track that led into the woods behind the lake.

When he stepped out of the car, he heard a whip-poor-will call. Farther in the distance, he heard the random barking of dogs. He took a deep breath, thought that he should have worn different shoes, and started walking on the path into the woods. He wondered if he should call out Bear's name in this lonely place. The trees rose up around him, taller here than in other places on Windy Creek, bent and thick, their branches imposing against the night sky. A half-moon appeared occasionally through the trees and made the bark on the cottonwoods look like a ghostly skin.

One thing Father Joe was sure about was that Bear knew these woods better than he did. Bear had no fear of them. He wasn't afraid of ticks or poison ivy, wild animals, whatever other creatures of the dark there were. He'd grown up out here. He knew how to take care of himself. Whereas Father Joe, for all of his years on the reservation, didn't know this place at all. He'd been to Ghost Lake maybe twice in all of these decades. He knew that Alice came out here with the kids in the early summer to look for a wild turnip that he could never remember the name of. "Don't worry, Father," Alice had said when he'd apologized for forgetting—again—the name of the root that she loved so much. "Sometimes the plants have to tell you their own names." He'd never been here at night. Never with a flashlight. He had an image of the tree roots reaching up for him. Of the trees bending ominously toward him.

He thought of a story he heard Alice tell once about what to listen for when you walked these wild, empty lands at night. "Listen," she said. "Because the footsteps of everyone who has ever walked here are with you. You will hear the bone fringes on their feet as they dance behind you. You will turn and look and they will not be there." This did not feel particularly comforting. He took it that Alice found it so, but he did not. But maybe, maybe it was a trick of his imagination that he could feel that ghostly presence, that silvery light that disappeared when you turned to look, like needles flashing in the dark.

When Father Joe had decided to become a priest, he had thought that it meant you got some kind of special knowledge, some map to live a life by. And not any map. Not the map everybody else got. A special map. God's map. It was possible that there were priests who found that map. He didn't know what it was like for them. For him, it felt like he wanted every day for directions he did not have. The effect was perhaps magnified on Windy Creek, where people very rarely used maps. Father Joe suspected that Rabbit's hasty sketch on the back of an envelope was a concession to him. To anyone else Rabbit would have said. "I got Ghost Lake to Sand Hill. You got Ghost Lake to Iron Shell Cabin," and everything would have been perfectly clear. If you got lost on Windy Creek and you asked directions, you got a vague mumble, something about up a hill and a certain tree and then, "You know, a ways down from there." There were almost no marked streets and only a few houses had numbers, and most of those were for show. The people felt that abstracting land like that—as white people did without thinking—was disrespectful. You had an obligation to know the land, not with a map but with your body and your spirit.

Once when he and Bear were down by the creek near Alice's house when Bear was about ten, Bear told him how to find an arrowhead. First he said, you have to climb to a high place. Then when you get there, you can't look for them. They won't come out if you look for them. You just have to ask for them and then let go.

"Is that right?" Father Joe had said.

"I found tons of them that way."

"You look without looking?"

"Kinda."

Father Joe had tried to imagine what this "look without looking" was like. What might you actually *do* when you are not looking?

"You'll have to take me sometime, show me how it's done."

"Maybe."

They hadn't gone, and now Father Joe couldn't remember if he hadn't followed through or if Bear had been evasive. He wished they had, anyway.

Without realizing it, Father Joe had started up the hill toward Gayle's lonely trailer. Once he recognized that he was heading that way, he thought he might at least stop by and see if the old man knew anything. And from the top of the hill, he could get a better lay of the land and try to understand what Rabbit had meant by "and west."

But when he reached the porch, he suddenly wasn't sure if he should wake Gayle or not. He sat down on one of the lawn chairs with a sigh and felt the ache in his knees.

He heard Gayle's voice call out, "Who's there?"

"It's me. Father Joe."

"Oh, wicasa wakan, it's you, is it?" He sighed as if he had been expecting this middle-of-the-night visit.

"I thought you might be asleep," Joe said.

"Old man, you know I don't sleep." He heard the creak of bed springs and a few minutes later, Gayle came out in a well-worn plaid bathrobe and moccasins. He sat down on the steps and looked out across the meadow that had bloomed with golden-rod, the shapes visible in the moonlight.

"And what brings you to my house at this hour?" he asked.

"It's Alice's boy, Bear. He's run off. She sent us out to look for him."

They sat in silence for a moment.

He grunted. "You don't seem to be looking too hard."

"If you want to find something," Father Joe said, "do you really send a priest to look for it?"

Gayle grunted again.

"It's nice having a bit of company in the middle of the night. You should come by here more often."

They watched the moon glide higher.

"Wakalapi?"

"I've got to keep going. I can't stay."

"He'll come back," Gayle said. "You might as well go home and climb in your bed. No point in looking for what has to find itself."

Father Joe returned to the Buick in the dark before sunrise. He sat for a moment in the dark and quiet of the car and felt his exhaustion, the ache that ran from the arches of his feet to the top of his head. The night had been different from long nights he'd spent in the hospital with dying parishioners where the hum of the machines and the twenty-four-hour bustle and the endless cups of coffee created a buzz around the exhaustion. Here he felt both tired and something else, something he couldn't quite name. Yes, he was worried for Bear. Yes, he wanted Alice to think he'd done a good job, that she'd been right to trust him with the task. He'd found nothing, but even as he looked, he had realized he was looking for more than Bear. All night long the woods had been talking to him, telling him something. Even through his fear, he could almost hear it. A night spent in the woods was a very different kind of night indeed. It was as if the boy had taken him to look for arrowheads after all and had taught him how to look without looking.

A misty gray had risen above the lake. The all-night call of the whip-poor-will had stayed with him on endless repeat. That relentless bird. Poor Will indeed. There had been no sign of Bear. In the dark of the front seat, he clipped on his collar and drove to the hospital.

He found Alice by Jackie's bedside. Alice looked ravaged, gaunt, and even a little bent, like a woman he didn't know or a woman he would know in twenty years but not today, not this woman who had been his guide. The strongest, surest, bravest woman of them all. If you want to destroy a woman, go after her children. Pick them off one by one.

She looked at him with a question in her eyes, and he shook his head. "I came straight here," he said. "I haven't checked in with the others. Why don't you go do that and I'll stay?"

She nodded and touched his shoulder and left.

He took a seat and closed his eyes, then thought: coffee. They must have some in the waiting room, and maybe he could ask someone all the questions that Alice had left unanswered. Jackie was quiet and unmoving on the bed. She had an IV and an oxygen tube in her nose. Monitors blinked on and off near her head with an occasional beeping sound that made him glance toward the dancing lines as if they might tell him what he wanted to know. He studied the bruises on her face and a crack along the bowl of her right eye that was held together with stitches. They had shaved part of her hair and there were stitches there as well—a deep gash wound that had been made by a heavy object. There were bruises on her arms, some that looked older than others. And around her neck. Someone had been very intent about their business. Still through all that machinery and monstrous markings, all of those bruises, he could still see the shy shape of her, the lightness, the girl a delicate question mark.

He stood and went into the bright hallway. In the waiting room, he found the coffee machine and poured himself a cup, adding powdered creamer because he didn't expect the coffee to be any good here, but it might be enough to get him through. He paused to take a sip and then turned to go back toward Jackie's room. The nurse was not at the nursing station, and the questions he most wanted answered he didn't think would be answered by her anyway. As he turned, he saw Bear. Lightning quick, as if trying to get from one door to another without being seen but moving in the direction of Jackie's room. He was alone. Father Joe almost cried out, but then he decided to wait. The boy had a purpose, and Father Joe was surprised to find that he had some trust for it. Not full trust. Not confidence. But a whisper that said, "Leave it be." *There's no point looking for what has to find itself,* Gayle had said.

He walked slowly toward Jackie's room, wondering if he should use the hospital phone to try Alice at home. When he got to the door, he saw Bear inside kneeling by the side of Jackie's bed, resting his head against the rails. His hand rested on her hand above him. Father Joe couldn't tell if he was praying or crying or sleeping.

7

Paperwork

VINCENT HAD BEEN helicoptered to Rapid City with stab wounds to his back. The knife, which the police now had in a baggie at the police station, was his own. The pearl inlay, fancy blade, can't-never-be-too-careful knife.

Many of the other details were hidden with Jackie and Bear, who seemed to have come to some kind of pact not to talk. Alice tried, along with the police, to piece things together. Mabel Beaufort, who lived next door, had called the police. She had one of the only phones in the whole building. But it was clear she had called them about the fight between Vincent and Jackie, and not about Bear. "Those two fought like the devil," she told the police. She was going to have to move, she said when she learned about the stabbing. She couldn't keep living there picturing that man lying on the floor in his own blood. "Stabbed," she said several times. "You would hear them screaming at each other in the night. You would hear things falling over. Since they moved in, it's been nothing but trouble. I kept telling Jacy Two Elk, this is not going to end well. You ask her. I told her many times."

Once the police had given Father Joe and Alice the all clear, they had gone over to the apartment to collect Jackie's things. There was still yellow tape across the metal screen door. The apartment smelled of cigarettes and old grease. There were beer bottles on the counter next to the sink and ashtrays in the living room with stubs. In the bedroom, a lamp was turned over on its side on the floor and the police had marked off part of the carpet where there were bloodstains. The bed was unmade, and the room had a stale smell.

Alice was steely and quiet as she pulled clothes from the closet and stuffed them into the duffel bag she had brought. "We don't want much, Father. Maybe we can just leave most of this for now." She looked around as though trying to picture the scene that had brought them here.

"What in God's name did she see in him?" Father Joe picked up a pair of Jackie's shoes from the floor and handed them to Alice.

"He was a force," Alice said. "I am not saying that explains it."

"He was like a planet with a gravitational pull."

"We all felt it."

"Do you think he'll come back?" Father Joe asked.

"You mean, if he lives?" She sighed. "I wouldn't put it past him. I wonder if we'll hear. I mean, if he gets out of the hospital. If he dies. Will they think to tell us?" She shuddered a little, as if she already felt his presence close by.

They didn't go into the living room. They'd come in through the back door into the kitchen and gone straight through to the bedroom. They went out the same way, glancing into the shadowed living room without speaking.

———

The police said the bloody fingerprints on the knife were Bear's. He'd dropped the knife, they said, and left Vincent to die on the faded, threadbare carpet of the living room. They traced bloody footprints out the front door and bloody fingerprints on the handle. The stabber had fled that way.

No one, however, could place Bear at the scene of the crime.

No one, including Jackie, so she said, remembered him being there that night, and he hadn't had anything to say about it. He'd gone deep inside himself, as if the events, whatever they had been, had thoroughly spent him and he didn't have the reserve to talk about them. Alice had tried gently a few times but had gotten nowhere. Father Joe had brought him a new sketchbook and gone to sit with him at the creek, but he wasn't talking.

Now the police wanted a formal interview with Bear. They were cagey about Vincent's condition, but they wanted to get an interview into their report. They weren't ready to file charges, and Alice wondered aloud if they were waiting for Vincent to die so they could charge Bear with murder.

"I don't see a way around it," Alice told Father Joe. "I said, 'I'd like to make it for some time after school so he doesn't have to miss class.' I tried to make it sound like he was a good student, but the truth is, he hasn't gone a single day since the year started."

Jackie had shaved all the hair off her head, and she looked both fierce and fragile. The scar glowed red through black stubble. She told the police that she didn't remember anything about that night except that she and Vincent had fought; he'd had a lot to drink. He'd picked up a lamp, and that was the last thing she remembered until she woke up in the hospital. "Bear wasn't there," she told the police when they'd come to interview her at the hospital. Maybe he'd come by the apartment a few times since they'd moved in, but it wasn't that common. "When they asked how Bear's fingerprints ended up on the knife, she'd offered, "Vincent let him hold that knife sometimes." The words felt weak, even if they were true.

———

Father Joe drove to the tribal police station with Alice and Bear. In the few minutes to the low, cinder block building along the highway, Bear sat slouched in the back seat looking out the window. The county sheriff's office was taking over the investigation, but they'd agreed to have the interview on Windy Creek. "This time," they'd said ominously, as if there were going to be many other times.

"A man has been stabbed," the sheriff's deputy had said to them, as if by way of explanation. An awkward opening to say the least, Father Joe thought. If he was trying to start a conversation, this was definitely not the way. The lines around Alice's mouth had set themselves into the clay of a mask. Like Bear, she was using as few words as possible. The deputy was white, Father Joe observed. Probably lived in Hanson. There were deep pouches under his eyes and a general sag about his jowls.

As Father Joe sat in the waiting area outside the office the tribal police had turned over to the sheriff's deputy, he tried to remember that this man was a professional. He saw what had happened through the lens of a "case." There were clues. There was evidence. It was his job to piece things together to make a whole. That whole would take the form of a report. At some point, he would turn the case over to the courts, and there would be more paperwork and more reports. Maybe what he saw when he looked at Bear across the desk was the need for paperwork. Maybe he was crafting the sentences that he would write on the report even as he talked with Bear. Father Joe judged that the man had a sloppy demeanor. His shirt was a little untucked. His shave was less than perfect, the mustache uneven. Father Joe wondered if he'd been criticized for poor paperwork in the past. That might account for his slight jumpiness, as if he were determined to get the upper hand right away but was actually nervous and out of place. He seemed like the kind of person who'd learned to cover up his insecurity with an excessive gruffness of style.

Alice and Bear were behind the office's glass, and Father Joe could only see their backs. From his position on an awkward plastic chair, he watched the man's jowls move up and down and observed that, for an interview, the man seemed to be doing most of the talking. That was no surprise. Every once in a while he would take out a piece of paper from the folder lying on the desk and gesture toward it, maybe even take a ripe finger and pound it down a few times on the paper, as if explaining something of great significance. He had a legal pad out. Maybe he'd meant to take some notes. Father Joe watched Bear's shoulders move up and down in his characteristic shrug, eyes on the floor.

Father Joe composed a speech to the man in his head. He wanted to explain to the man about Vincent, and the way that Vincent carried some aura about Albert's death like cigarette smoke. He wanted to explain about Alice, about family and her understanding of it, and about Bear's important, but mysterious, appearance in their lives. He wanted to say to the man, "Albert was special. He was beautiful. He wasn't just another Indian for you to round up and put in jail. If you want to do something useful, figure out who killed him. That's the real case here." But that speech didn't seem likely to help. And why was he bringing Albert into this? This was about Bear, about saving Bear's skin, since that wasn't something Bear was likely to do for himself.

When they came out, Alice squared her shoulders and put a hand on Bear's back. The deputy had said they were going ahead with charges of attempted murder in the second degree, she told Father Joe later when Bear had gone down to the creek with his sketchbook. They were trying to decide if they were going to charge him as a juvenile or an adult. "An adult?" Father Joe repeated. Alice shook her head. And they were trying to decide if he was going to be charged in tribal court or in the county system.

Bear was drawing again, as if whatever he had to say was going to be found there, with pencil and paper. He was drawing for many hours, Alice said when she and Father Joe sat together at the kitchen table with cups of coffee.

She didn't say much about the interview except to report to

Father Joe a piece of the deputy's advice. He'd told Bear, "When you do see a judge, I recommend that you look him in the eye, young man. When you look down, you look suspicious."

———

"That's absurd," Father Joe said into the phone. He was standing in Alice's kitchen a week later with papers spread out around them on the table.

The questions as they multiplied had begun to swirl around this one: how to get a birth certificate for Bear. For the first thirteen years of his life, they had not needed one. The question had come up when he was enrolled in school, but it was quickly set aside. Alice had said, "Yes, of course, I'll bring it in," and then no one thought about it again.

But you can't prove that someone was born retrospectively, except for the strange fact that the person in question is alive.

"What about if you fill in all those blanks with 'unknown'?" Father Joe asked the person on the other end. "You can have some of them be unknown," she said. "But you can't have all of them be unknown. For example, if you have a mother's name."

"He has a mother's name."

"But you said that this is not his birth mother."

"But it's a name. You can put it on the certificate."

"If she is a birth mother, then she would know other things, like where, what day, and what time he was born."

"He was born October twenty-second. Maybe twenty-third. Twenty-third latest. 1970. He was definitely born on Windy Creek."

"But not in the hospital?"

This was how the conversations went—around and around without those little necessary things, like facts. Father Joe was irritated with himself for not having insisted all those years ago that they do basic things—like get a birth certificate. And he was irritated with all of these petty demands. Just put something on the piece of paper and send it to us, he wanted to tell the woman on the other line. I don't care what it is. Facts are not essential here. We have bigger fish to fry.

But facts were her realm of significance. Facts were what she did every day. She verified facts. She put facts on paper.

The threat of an attempted murder charge was horrifying, but almost worse was a threat that had risen up alongside it: that Bear would become a ward of the state. The years of Alice's love counted for nothing when it came to filling in blanks. You couldn't write "loved beyond reason and without question" on a birth certificate.

It wasn't entirely clear to Father Joe why their inability to get a birth certificate would lead to Bear becoming a ward of the state. By what progression of logic? By whose desire? No one had need of that. The state didn't need one more child in the foster care system. Anyone could see with a quick glance that Bear was fine where he was, that his best shot through all of this and to a positive future was with Alice. But that was not the question. The question was: Where was Bear born? Hiding under that was another question: Was Bear Indian? Was he a member of the tribe? Could he apply for tribal membership? Tribal courts couldn't have jurisdiction over cases involving non-Indians. This principle was more important than anything having to do with Bear's life or future. Without knowing something about his mother and his father, they couldn't know the answer.

"Isn't that he was born here enough?" Alice asked. But it was not enough.

The bureaucrats, with their sometimes jolly and sometimes crisp voices, followed a logic of power first and foremost. Sometimes, Father Joe would hang up and then call whatever agency back again, just to start the conversation over with a different person who might have access to a different logic. He needed someone who could think slightly outside the box, someone who could be a creative partner, but whenever he said something like "Can you work with me here?" the voice on the other end grew tighter and he could see their chances diminishing in a flash.

Father Joe hung up the phone.

Alice had the note from Bear's mother open on the table, the faded blue ink, the perfect B.

"If only she had signed it," Alice said. Alice's hands were wrapped around a coffee mug that had quilt patterns on it, the kind they sold as Indian kitsch at Willie's Market along with factory-produced dream catchers and leather-cord key chains. The mug Alice had poured Father Joe's coffee into said SHE LOVES ME BEST. One of the children must have given it to her as a joke, purchased from the same place. It seemed like an Albert joke. He was the one who was sly like that.

Father Joe started talking emphatically. "I mean, what if there is some kind of statutory law for children like there is for property. Remember that man who lived for seven years in the shack on Moyer Ranch? Remember how they said that he'd lived there for seven years so technically the shack was his? Shouldn't there be a rule that if a child lives with you all their life, after a certain point, they are yours and it doesn't matter who else's they might have been once upon a time?"

"Speaking of which . . ." Alice sighed. "I've got calls into a couple of lawyers, but so far no one has called me back." Her eyes looked at Joe with a mix of sadness and curiosity.

"By the way," she said. "I heard you had a visitor."

"Word does get around here."

"What was it like?"

Father Joe studied the table in front of him. The linoleum top was peeling from one corner and there were an abundance of scratch marks, like a secret code waiting to be deciphered. He knew he was blushing, but there wasn't anything he could do about it.

"She has five kids," he said finally. "And two grandkids."

"Will you see her again?"

Joe was still looking down, but when he glanced up, she was smiling and the lines around her mouth deepened.

"We really need to get a lawyer," he said.

"Yes, we do."

8

Heaven and Earth

September 14, 1983

Dear Joseph,

I am sorry I barged in on you like that. I wanted to see you, but now I am a little chagrined about how I put you on the spot. That wasn't fair. I didn't even know I was going to come. I got up that morning. It was early. The sky was purple and tangerine. I got dressed and got in the car and was driving before I fully recognized what I was up to. It was easy to find you, though: that little church up on the hill. It was just like I pictured it. Or maybe it was that photograph from the Midwest Catholic Reporter. I guess it wasn't my own imagination.

It's interesting what's happening to me these days. My days have always been so circumscribed. For decades, there would have been absolutely no way I could have gotten in a car and driven anywhere, let alone across the state. I was always managing everyone's schedules: who had choir practice, who had band practice. And all the sports! Volleyball and softball and basketball. It went on and on, these seasons of demand. Church, dinner, lunches, groceries, a relentless cycle without any real need on my part to introduce anything other than organization. Keep it organized, that's what I did.

And now suddenly, nothing. My calendar is empty unless I go out of my way to fill it. I have choices, and I don't even know how to make them. I think that's one of the things that propelled me into the car that Sunday: the mere fact that I could do it and no one would stop me. An unadulterated moment of freedom. I felt like a teenager when I pulled out onto I-90.

It was nice to try to find again the kind of conversation you and I used to have. I want you to know that I've never talked with anyone like that again. And we had a hint of it at your table, didn't we? Just a hint.

But now it is all tangled up with all of these other lives we are living. We didn't know what a simple, good thing that was.

One thing I think is happening now in the quiet aftermath of my life as a mother is that I am becoming a contemplative! You'll laugh. But I sometimes pretend I am Thomas Merton in his little hermitage. I take my books and my notebooks out to the three-season porch and I try to imagine what Merton might be working on. A book on prayer? Well, I'm not quite there yet. Maybe a book on choice. I think I will write a book about free will, from a female perspective, from my own life experience. Maybe I will call it Free Will: The Myth of a Male-Dominated Church. Oh, so I am becoming both a contemplative and a feminist. I suppose I won't be able to get the bishop's approval for that one.

Well, I hope I didn't put you in a bad place. Tell me what your favorite books on free will are so that I can start reading them during my Merton Hours.

Sincerely,
Veronica

September 20, 1983

Dear Veronica,

Sometimes I imagine entering your life while leaving it entirely intact. The way, maybe, an image from a dream can disturb the depths but not affect the surface of a person's life. I want you to stay exactly as you are, with your husband's love and your children's admiration all without change. I have done such damage in the past by not finding the right way between action and in-action. I'm all fire or all ash, it seems.

I have this sensation that I have entered many rooms in my life wondering if you might be there. I've looked around for you, and I've felt this hint of disappointment, on the edge of my knowing, that you weren't there and weren't coming.

I crave knowing more about you. I crave the stories of your life. I want them told to me on the phone in the middle of the night or held in some utterly private space the two of us could make outside the ordinary flow of life.

But this is what I wanted when we were young, too, and now I know this would be a betrayal. There is no way to create this intrusion. It is a fantasy. But I turn it over and over tenderly in my mind.

About free will, most of what I've read—and it's been a while— feels archaic, like the old men are sitting around debating the degree of dryness in the sand. The old debates—the unmoved mover, the effect of grace and the effectiveness of grace—I'll tell you that from here, when I look around and I see the choices people make and the choices they don't, the effectiveness of grace doesn't come into play much. Mostly you want people to make one good choice—one choice for their own good or for the good of others. And they don't. But then sometimes one self-destructive act, done for the good of others or at least their imagined good, reverberates out and threatens to consume us all. How does that

make sense in the debates? How would good old Domingo Báñez
make sense of that one?

Sincerely,
Joseph

———————

September 28, 1983

Dear Joseph,

I suppose that this will sound rude and ungrateful, but I have
given this a lot of thought, and I want you to know that I am
saying these words without self-pity or without wishing it were
otherwise. He doesn't love me. He loves a very long-standing idea
of me. It is duty mixed with honor mixed with habit. It passes for
love, but I for one will not give it that name.

Sincerely,
Veronica

———————

In the mail with Veronica's letter was also a letter from the
bishop. He was coming in October. He wanted to sit down with
Father Joe and talk through some things. He'd come midweek,
his letter said, if that would work. No hustle and bustle. None of
the usual pomp and circumstance, although if Father Joe had
anyone who needed confirmation, he would rethink it and try
to get there for a Sunday. Or maybe they could schedule that for
the beginning of the year.

———————

The bishop pulled up in his black Cadillac and parked it next to
the Buick outside the rectory. No bishop had been to the reservation in a few years, even though a yearly visit was the standard.
This bishop was new. The one before had been moved to Kansas

City. Father Joe didn't think of himself as much on the bishop's radar—something he had learned to appreciate and not be offended by. On the radar by and large meant trouble. Under the radar meant, Father Joe told himself, that you were doing your job. Under the radar meant not adding any extra problems to the ones you already had. That's partly why Veronica's comment about the "famous Father Kreitzer" made him nervous.

Lydia had not been happy that the bishop was coming and that her instructions were not to do anything special. She'd looked at Father Joe hard, even a little angry, and then had bustled around like she hadn't heard him, banging pots and pans. In the end, she'd made a pineapple upside-down cake and left it on the counter in the kitchen under a glass cover, little red cherries dotting the browned pineapple in syrup. As a peace offering, Father Joe had told her it looked really nice.

The two men sat in the rectory's rarely used living room, where the furniture was stiff and formal, from another era. The furniture evoked an idea of priesthood that Father Joe thought didn't hold together particularly well, at least not for reservation life. But it was someone's idea of the priesthood, of a rectory, and maybe back in the day it had held a meaning Father Joe couldn't discern from where he sat.

Father Joe had poured them glasses of Scotch, and the bishop kept the tone light. He told Father Joe about a confirmation class he was running out of the cathedral. There was one boy, he said, who was making things especially hard. He'd come to see the bishop to tell him that he didn't think he should be confirmed because he didn't actually believe any of this stuff. The boy wore shoes without socks, even in winter, and his feet had a smell that the boy didn't recognize. Or maybe he recognized it, and he liked it. To make things worse, the boy's father taught at the Catholic high school and his mother was in mass every morning.

"I asked him what he did believe in, and he said 'Science,' like that was something you could believe in." The bishop snorted a little.

"What did you tell him?"

"I told him that some of the greatest men of the church were scientists and that there was no necessary contradiction between science and faith."

"What did he say to that?"

"He said, 'Galileo.'" They both laughed. Father Joe couldn't tell what was in his own laughter. Maybe it was the boy's candor and simplicity, his courage to speak to the bishop what he actually thought and even to present a challenge to a person who probably went through most of his days without being challenged.

"In the end I told him belief wasn't everything. We change. We grow. Our beliefs evolve, especially at his age. I told him the church had enough room for his skepticism. 'Let's get you confirmed,' I said, 'and then we can keep talking.'"

"So it was a success, then?"

"Well, in a manner of speaking. He thought I was patronizing him, which I probably was. He thought I was trying to talk him into doing something nice for his folks. And again, he wasn't wrong. But he went through with it, and everyone was happy, except maybe him."

The bishop before this one had been the first part-Indian bishop in the Dakotas. This one was cut from a more familiar cloth. The previous bishop had been a quarter Cherokee, and the diocese had made a big deal about it. On top of that, he'd been really good at finding his way between heaven and earth. He'd had an instinct for it, an instinct that was hard to see in the man who now sat across from him. This man had instincts, for sure, but they did seem more earth-oriented. But things had gone wrong for the previous bishop as early as his installation, when he'd asked a holy man to come and give a blessing but he'd overlooked the fact that the man was Crow, not Lakota, and the Lakota had not really forgiven the Crow for spying for Custer. It was rocky.

After a second glass of Scotch, the bishop finally told Father Joe what he'd come for: they were going to close St. Rose. It was a period of consolidation, he said. It was happening all over the state, all over the country really. They were taking a hard look at their finances and deciding where they could cut back. It didn't make much sense to have such a small parish here when there was a larger one ten miles down the road in High Horse. Father Joe's people could easily go over there. Now with Blessed Sacrament, the school, no longer being run by the church, the church had more capacity. It didn't make sense to do all the repairs that Father Joe had put in for and keep these smaller parishes running. They were expensive propositions.

"You know, we are doing good work here."

"We know, we know. You've done a great service, Kreitzer. You've done what no one else could have done, and you've got a lot of fans. We're proud as hell of you."

"And next?" Father Joe asked. He tried to keep his face steady.

"There's a parish in Hastings, Nebraska, where we think you could really do some good things."

"Hastings, Nebraska?" Father Joe swallowed hard. "What's your timeline?"

"We're thinking after the first of the year."

"I need until Easter," Father Joe said, thinking fast.

"Fine. Settled before Pentecost then."

9

A Place in the Family of Things

A DATE HAD BEEN SET in tribal court for a few days after Bear's birthday, and while they waited, Bear stayed out of school and mostly by the creek with his sketchbook. His silence had deepened and expanded. You could almost wade in it. Father Joe watched the boy mature through silence, so different, he thought, than how most boys matured. They talked and joked and razzed each other. He had driven Albert to Rapid City once when he was Bear's age with a couple other boys. Maybe to take them to a video arcade for a birthday or something. He couldn't remember now. What he remembered was that the boys had sat in the back of the Buick and giggled for hours. They found everything funny and couldn't stop laughing. Bear wasn't like that. He was inside himself and getting him out was going to be a challenge.

There were so many questions that Father Joe wanted to ask him about that night. He'd taken the pad by the phone in the rectory and written them out: Were you at the apartment? Where was Jackie when you arrived? Did you come in through the front door or through the back? Where was the knife? Where was Vincent standing? Did you act in self-defense? Did you act at all or was there someone else there—someone whose name you are refusing to give us? Where did you go when you left and why did you leave?

Father Joe hoped that someone in the police investigation was at least asking these questions, but the police seemed a little more absorbed with the question of jurisdiction. The first question the tribal judge had to settle was whether Bear's case could be heard on Windy Creek at all. They'd found a lawyer, a young man who had graduated from the University of South Dakota law school and was having his loans forgiven by taking on cases like Bear's. He looked so young to Father Joe that he didn't find himself filled with confidence. "What was he? Fifteen?" he said to Alice. But he at least knew what motions to file and how to file them. His plan for them on the day of court was to plead for more time to research Bear's standing with the tribe. If Bear was not a member of the tribe, then the case would move to federal jurisdiction, not something any of them wanted. But the laws that were clear about few things were clear on this one: the federal government executed all jurisdiction over any cases involving non-Indians against Indians. Period. So if Bear was not a member of the tribe, then his case would be handled in federal court.

The slightly murkier area involved Bear's status as a juvenile. Technically, all juvenile cases were handled in federal court, but if Bear was Indian, then there was good reason to argue that the case could stay within the tribal system. It was a tangled mess anyway. Father Joe had driven to the state library in Pierre and spent hours looking up what he could in the *South Dakota Law Review* and the *American Indian Law Review*, trying to find any similar cases. With the birth certificate question still looming, the lawyer said the family could ask for more time.

When Father Joe arrived at the cinder block building on the court date, Alice and Bear were standing outside. They were both wearing their hair in long braids down their backs, and Joe found himself wondering if they had discussed ways for Bear to look more Indian. Alice was wearing intricately beaded earrings in turquoise and yellow—like suns.

The lawyer pulled up in a bright blue Honda Civic with a sunroof, and Father Joe looked at it admiringly. You didn't see many foreign cars on the reservation—certainly few things that were sporty like this little thing was. The lawyer unfolded himself from the interior of the car like unbending a straw. He had a hurried look about him. His hair was slightly messy and he was still straightening his tie, trying, Father Joe imagined, to look lawyerly.

As they went inside together, the lawyer leaned toward Bear and whispered, "No need to say anything today. The important thing today is that you're here, showing your face. That's it. Otherwise you'll have your chance to speak later on. Today I am going to make a motion. The judge will decide on that, and that's it. It shouldn't even be five minutes."

The heavy, polished wood of the courtroom looked like it belonged to another place, like it had been borrowed and set up here in the low-ceilinged, cinder block room. Alice, Father Joe, Bear, and the lawyer sat together in the back while the clerk read out cases and people came and went. Drunk driving, simple assault, petty theft.

Finally the clerk said, "The court calls the case of Bernard Nighthawk." They moved forward, following the tall, thin lawyer to the front. Bernard and Alice sat at one of the tables, and Father Joe took a place behind them.

The judge looked to the tribe's lawyer. He was a middle-aged man with a head of curls and thick dark eyebrows. Father Joe remembered reading about him during the Wounded Knee occupation, making a name for himself then. Father Joe noticed the black hairs on the back of his hand and that he a habit of clearing his throat repeatedly.

He read out the basics of the case. "A charge of voluntary

manslaughter in the second degree has been brought against Bernard Nighthawk, age thirteen. Details of the case have brought to light a question about tribal jurisdiction. At this time, we are asking to have the case removed to federal court because Bernard Nighthawk is not a member of the Lakota Sioux Tribe and so this court has no jurisdiction over his case."

The judge looked out at them over a pair of half-rimmed glasses with a paper in his hand that no doubt said the things that the lawyer had spoken.

"Your Honor," Bear's lawyer said. "We are asking for more time to investigate the question of Bernard Nighthawk's enrollment as a member of the tribe."

"You are aware that the tribal courts have no jurisdiction over criminal prosecution of non-Indians?"

"We are, Your Honor."

"Birth certificate?"

"We are looking for it."

"Social security card?"

"No."

"Tribal records?"

"No."

"How did this boy come to be in the custody of this woman?"

Father Joe could feel tension running through Alice, as if she'd been plugged into a socket.

"Your Honor, we will make a full report to the court when we've had sufficient time to study the matter."

"What about a baptism certificate?" The judge looked up over his glasses at me. The lawyer nodded at me.

"Yes, your honor. There is a certificate of baptism."

"What's the date of birth?"

"October twenty-third, 1970."

"Parents?"

"Alice Nighthawk is listed as his mother."

The judge looked down at his papers again. The tribe's lawyer cleared his throat as if he were going to speak, but Father Joe recognized it was a tic.

"Do you have any idea the consequences?" The judge was looking directly at Alice. "Even if this . . . event . . . had never happened, what were your plans? How would a boy get a job without a birth certificate? How would he enroll in college? Are you aware that the state could make a case that you kidnapped this boy?"

Father Joe could see the side of Alice's face as she turned toward the lawyer. Her mouth had drawn into a very thin, straight line. Please hurry, he thought hard in the direction of the lawyer. This could get ugly.

"Your Honor," the lawyer said, "we are working on these things, and we believe we have what is necessary to officially enroll the boy in the tribe. We need a little more time. We believe there is good reason for the case to be heard on Windy Creek."

The judge turned to the tribe's lawyer. His briefcase was open, packed with folders, and he was shuffling through them.

"Objections?" the judge asked.

"None," the man said.

The judge turned to the clerk. "Put it on the docket for April. Let's do a check-in on the progress in early December. Next case."

———

"What now?" They stood together in the parking lot in front of the courthouse. The October wind swirled cottonwood leaves around them.

"It's simple," Alice said. "We are going to find her." She looked at Bear, who was kicking at leaves with his foot, and she put an arm around him to draw her to him. Father Joe had not realized until that moment that he was now taller than Alice. The gesture to embrace him looked awkward, like he had grown not only above but also away from her.

"Who?" Father Joe asked.

"Bear's mother."

Alice faced everything the same way she faced the wind: straight on. It was as if she saw the face of Bernard's mother right out in front of her, perhaps ahead of her on some path, turning slightly in her direction. All she had to do was go toward that face and it would reveal itself to her.

But the courtroom had brought out one of her deepest fears. More than any wind or rain or tornado or ice storm or blinding blizzard, Alice feared paperwork. File folders and reports. She didn't trust the system that held her children too often in its hand. "Their books," she had named this fear when Bear had first come to them, and she had asked Father Joe not to call the authorities. She had done everything she knew how to do to keep Bear out of their books. She had given him what she believed he truly needed: the knowledge of his place in the family of things. And yet here they were facing briefcases full of papers.

"This is simple," she said again as they turned toward their cars. "We probably already know her. She's been watching us all along. All we have to do is let her know we need her, and she will come to us."

———

"You know the one place where we never really looked?" Alice was rapping her pen on the linoleum table. "Blessed Sacrament. I mean I called them, but when they said they had nothing, I dismissed it. We never really looked there. Why did I actually think they were telling me the truth?"

She was looking away from Father Joe toward the door, as if the answer might walk through it.

Father Joe had not told her yet that the bishop was going to close St. Rose and send him to Hastings, Nebraska. He was counting the finality of the seasons in front of them: this would be their last Advent, their last Christmas, their last Lent, their last Easter. He hadn't told anybody.

"Could it be," Father Joe said. "Because we weren't really that interested in finding her?"

Alice gave him a soft glare across the table and stood up to turn on the stove.

"What do you think happened," Alice said, "to all the paperwork that the school had when they turned it over to the tribe? Did the priests take all of that with them or did they leave it at the school?"

Father Joe pictured the old stone building of the school. It looked overgrown and abandoned in the oak grove. There were broken windows, and it had the air of a haunted house, as if no one wanted to touch it or deal with it or even tear it down. It was encased in silence. He wondered if there were boxes of files in the basement or a filing cabinet somewhere that had BLESSED SACRAMENT MISSION SCHOOL written on masking tape on the front, but no one ever opened the drawers.

"It's lucky," Alice said as she started to chop an onion and drop it into the pan on the stove. "Because if the priests have the records, you can get them. And if the Indians have the records, I can get them."

"Records of what, though?"

"Girls. We are looking for girls. Girls who ran away. Girls who went missing. Girls who suddenly stopped showing up for class. Maybe there's some reference to 'trouble' a girl got in. Maybe there are letters or discipline records. We'll read through them all. This'll be easy. I mean, what are we talking: 1969–1970. It's nothing. A few months."

"I wish you wouldn't keep saying that this will be easy. It doesn't seem easy to me at all."

"What do you want me to say?"

The two of them looked at each other for a moment. Alice held a spatula. Father Joe shut his pen and put it into his shirt pocket.

"Do you know the Lakota words for children, Father?"

"Sure, I do. It's . . ." Father Joe struggled with the multitude of words in Lakota for relations. They were so many and so complex. There were words for children in relation to women and in relation to men and in relation to women who were relations and men who were relations. Direct address and indirect address. Kinds, qualities, quantities of relation. Father Joe could handle a nice thick lexicon and a list of words. He didn't mind nuances in meanings. But there was no Klein for Lakota. The language didn't work that way. It had a different logic, and one that was opaque to him.

"Wakan ye ja. Do you know what that means?" She paused, in case he wanted to jump in. "They are too sacred."

PART II

Where Secrets Are Kept

WINDY CREEK RESERVATION,

SOUTH DAKOTA

1983–1984

10

Qol

HE HAD PROMISED ALICE he would call the diocese and ask where school records from the late '60s and early '70s were kept. He'd ask if he could visit the filing cabinets. That was a promise he intended to keep. But the moment she was asking about and wanted them to probe—for Bear's sake, he reminded himself, all of this is for Bear—was perhaps the second most painful moment in his career. The first was that wordless dismissal of Rossling's at St. Martin's in the spring of 1958, that sense that he was nothing more than a stray hair on Rossling's trousers to be disposed of at will. But this one was close.

In the summer of 1970, Father Joe had been in Willie's Market when he'd looked up and seen a man he had hoped never to see again. He and Flynn had both been working under Rossling at St. Martin's. Not friends. The staff was big; there was always a lot going on. So they'd sat around tables together, taken turns at the coffee machine, been in mass together dozens of times. Flynn was lean and balding—he'd already been losing his hair ten years before—with big round glasses that made his eyes look bigger than they were. ("The better to see you with, my dear," Joe thought.) At Willie's he was wearing a priest's collar and buying a package of Twinkies and a bag of peanut M&M's.

Father Joe loitered near the coffee machine to let the man pass out the glass doors toward the parking lot. He realized that he had started sweating and his collar felt tight and hot.

"You okay, Father J?" Josie, who worked the cash register, asked. "You don't look so good."

Father Joe pulled a napkin out of the dispenser and wiped his face with it. It was hot, well over ninety degrees, with dark clouds building up in the west.

"I think I just got a little overheated's all," he said.

When he'd gotten back to his office, he tried to decide what to do. Should he call Father Fabian and casually ask about new staff at the school? Was there any other reason that Flynn might be here? Was there another parish in the area where he might have been called? Maybe he was just passing through, on a road trip. Father Joe thought maybe he'd call the bishop and say "What the hell? Get that guy out of here!"

That's what he had done all those years ago in Rossling's office. He'd barged in, certain he'd be heard if his voice was loud enough. He'd come away ashamed, having seen in Rossling's eyes first a flash of fear and then watching while fear was overcome with officiousness, and he knew he had failed. A bumbler's move. He told Rossling what he thought he'd seen that man do, who he'd seen that man with. "Can you be sure?" Rossling had asked. "Well, no, it was just a moment, but . . ." Rossling had said, "You've been working so hard, Kreitzer. Maybe you need a retreat. We could arrange something for you." But instead of a retreat, Rossling went silent, and the next thing Father Joe knew he was on his way to Windy Creek without so much as a final meeting. Whatever Father Joe had done, whatever he had stirred, they'd gotten rid of him quickly, hadn't they?

But Flynn was in his territory now. Father Joe was more than ten years in. He'd set up a food pantry at the community center; they'd started a Society of St. Vincent de Paul. People thought he was getting things right—righter than usual anyway. He had some authority now. Maybe they'd listen to him. It was true that as the years had gone by, he'd become less and less sure of what he thought he'd seen. It'd been more of a feeling, he realized. He could understand why Rossling had been quick to dismiss it.

At the same time, it didn't take a whole lot of reasoning to figure out why Flynn was on the reservation. He was being punished for something. That's what they did: sent people to Windy Creek for punishment. They wanted to scare the shit out of him. But he shouldn't be here. He shouldn't be at the school. He shouldn't be buying M&M's. They should've long since gotten that guy stuffed away in an office somewhere where he couldn't do any harm.

What Father Joe felt more than any other thing—more than the rage and the fear that had overtaken him at Willie's—was helplessness. There was nothing he could do, and he knew it. He felt an ache in his arms and in his chest that said "You're already beat, Joe, and you haven't even started." It wasn't a clear voice. It was more ache than words, and a panic rising.

He was still sweating in his office, sweating through his shirt. He pulled his handkerchief out of his pocket and mopped his face again.

Now in his office again, thirteen years farther on, Flynn having come and gone from the reservation so fast, it might only have been a moment in a nightmare. Fabian long gone too. Several bishops come and gone. And Father Joe still here.

It felt a little like a comfort to imagine that at the moment Flynn had arrived on the reservation, Veronica had said that she dreamed about him and had reached toward him. Then he remembered that she had also said that she had tried to reach him and couldn't.

He wasn't making a lot of progress on his translations these days. His mind was full of the complex Hebrew of federal, state, and tribal law more than the Hebrew of the psalms. But he wondered if he could just take a moment to hide himself. If, instead of reaching for the phone to call the diocese and ask about the filing cabinets, he might reach for the commentaries and the lexicons like a ballast. Did he dare lose himself there for an hour or two? Would it refresh him to be lost in mysteries, in the concrete and simultaneously ineffable? Maybe these were like Veronica's Merton Hours.

He laid out the whole of Psalm 50 before him. At first glance, it hinged on the word "voice"—qol, לוֹק—again three little letters, again evoking more than they appeared. On the legal pad, he traced the letters: qoph—sound. Vav—connection. Lamed—instruction.

In Hebrew, voice was always and everywhere inflected with "voice of God," as if all speech were divine in origin. God spoke the world into being. Every word spoken since has a direct connection to the first words, the divine speech. And here it was evoked in the first line of the psalm. On his legal pad, Joe traced a line from *qol* to the Greek word *logos*—the divine word that is present at the time of all creation. Jesus himself, the ancient texts say, was a form of divine speech. And that extended to everyone who shares the divine image: they speak and the world comes into being. What we say is. With our words, we create worlds. If that were true, why couldn't Alice speak Bear's mother into being, breathe her up from the ground?

He started in on the first line. *El Elohim*, even *Hashem. El*—a name for God. Then another name for God—*Elohim*, the plural for *El*. This was the name for the creator, evoking that first divine word: *In the beginning Elohim created the heavens and the earth.* Then *Hashem*, which means literally "the Name." So the text goes, God, God, the Name. If you heard it sung, Joe imagined, it might bring tears to your eyes, hearing these names for God, a melody full of longing for that which is and is not. It might feel like a prayer from the heart, a plaintive cry. A name that cannot be spoken. A word that doesn't yield with the saying.

But it suddenly seemed to Father Joe like a knock-knock joke.

"God."

"God who?"

"God God."

"God God who?"

"God God the Name"

"God God the Name who?"

And so you could go on, caught in some kind of endless cycle of naming and not naming because of the paradox that the voice had no name and yet the nameless name speaks.

Maybe this wasn't such a good day for translating after all. He got up and walked to the window, looking out across the meadow that was now brown and gold with dried stalks—squirrel-tail and rabbitbrush and smooth brome. Occasionally willows flashed red, swollen with the insect homes buried inside them.

Father Fabian came back to him at that moment, with the smell of his pipe tobacco and the squeak of his expensive shoes. He'd had a way of being so precise that you didn't dare question him. That natural authority he carried with him. It was a physical presence, a presence Father Joe had never had. There was always something slightly stumbling about Father Joe. But Fabian walked with elegance, with certainty and clarity, and could draw everyone along with him. An air of indisputability. That's what the old men in black, as Gayle called them, had wanted in a leader for the school in those days. They'd wanted someone who could at least pretend to right the ship and convince everyone it was righted. They didn't care so much if it was righted, so much as that it needed to have the sense of rightness. That's what they were all after: a sense of rightness. Therein was the problem. What looked right was wrong. What looked wrong was right.

Fabian hadn't been much older than Father Joe when he arrived. He'd been a chaplain in the military, which they liked. Blessed Sacrament had been in rough shape. It didn't look right, and it wasn't right. But he'd gotten the books in order. He'd gotten the teachers on board. He'd fixed certain disciplinary issues that had plagued the previous principal. The faculty fell in line. The parents stopped complaining. He said things like "There's a fine spirit at the school this year" and everyone believed him because he said it. Father Joe could still hear the way he said "fine," a lifting of the eyebrows, a leaning forward on the expensive shoes so that you could hear that distinctive squeak. Confounding. Frustrating. Those were the words that Father Joe had used when speaking to . . . well, to no one. No one had wanted to hear it. It had happened only in speeches that Father Joe would give to Fabian in his head. "Now you see here, things aren't quite as they seem," he would say silently.

Father Joe justified his silence by the very fact that Fabian would not listen to him. If you said "The dormitory is on fire!," Father Fabian would say, "Yes, well, thank you so much for your input. We've got that handled."

But the school had in fact gone down on his watch. A few years later, a group of parents and grandparents had approached the church and said, "We want to run this place ourselves." It was in the aftermath of Wounded Knee. Even though the action had all been on Pine Ridge, it had bled over and infected the relationship between the church and the people. There was no real need for a Father Fabian, truth be told. He was there to comfort the old men. But the people themselves had little use for him. The Jesuits, however, believed that the school wouldn't last a year after they left. They thought their good faith and diligence held the place together.

Father Joe had tried to find his voice in the midst of all of this. He'd gone over to see Father Fabian in the wood-paneled office, sat in a leather easy chair, accepted a glass of Scotch.

"Fabian," he'd said, "we need to talk about Flynn." He'd tried to be direct but not angry. He didn't want to see that Rossling look in Fabian's eyes. He wanted to do better this time. "He doesn't belong here. I knew him in Minnesota. This isn't a place for him. He doesn't belong around"—he'd paused here, trying to choose his words carefully—"children."

At first Fabian was circumspect. He held his cards close. "I deal with what they send me," he'd said, as if he were the post-master and Flynn were a package.

But the conversation had devolved, and anger had risen up in Father Joe until he had said, "You are holding on to a delusion, Fabian."

Fabian had turned away from Father Joe so that Father Joe could see his patrician profile, and he'd said quietly, "No one is more deluded than you, Kreitzer."

Father Joe had been so struck by it, so struck by what he might mean, by what the quality of his own delusion might be, that he'd dropped the subject. His German silence had overwhelmed him at that moment, the silence of his father and his grand-fathers, and he'd said to himself, perhaps wrongly, that there was nothing more to add. All fire or all ash, as he'd told Veronica.

Soon after, Fabian was packing and taking an administrative job in the diocese of Oregon. Flynn was off as well to some other place, where no doubt he wouldn't be for long. Father Joe had tried to keep his head down, in case they decided to close St. Rose while they were at it. He could do the most good, he rea-soned, by staying where he was.

11

Gone

November 4, 1983

Dear Joseph,

Today I got up early and watched the sun rise from the three-season porch, otherwise known as the Hermitage. In summer when I sit here, I watch for the first rays of the sun on the farthest stalks of the corn visible on the horizon. In November I wait as the sky changes through shades of gray, and I try to perceive each small shift in color. We built the porch some years ago to look south over the meadow and then toward the cornfields and the grain elevator. Now I sit out here in all kinds of weather. I've got a space heater and a stack of blankets.

The fields are plowed under now with rough, uneven stalks, brown and bent. No snow yet, so the ground is mutations of brown, like the sky is variations of gray.

When we first moved here, we thought about turning the meadow into a basketball court for the kids. It was an empty patch of land to us, and we thought we should do something with it. I don't know if I can adequately say how glad I am that we did not. That meadow is my salvation. On that "empty" patch of land I watch voles and muskrats and rabbits and all manner of birds. Sometimes I walk out there to see what I can scare up because there is always something. On the first Sunday of Advent, I go out to the meadow and collect little bits of grass and dried berries and anything that strikes me as beautiful. Have you ever really looked at the heads of grass in winter, Joseph? They are remarkable—the stark patterns and shapes, the range of colors and textures. I collect them and put them in little jars in the house. And then I wait for the first pasque flower in the spring like it is the second coming of Christ.

These are the things that I love, have loved, and can imagine loving forever. But there are other things that tug on me and make me think about what could be next for me. The pig farm across the road, for example, is expanding. And toward town, one of our neighbors sold his cornfield to a developer. Cornfields are going for a lot of money these days. So this little island is being closed in by a pig farm on one side and development on the other.

I spoke rashly of my marriage in my last letter, and maybe that's why you didn't answer. I keep stepping over one line after another in myself, and I keep wondering, "Where's the real boundary?" And sometimes "How could you? Who is this person who doesn't know how to behave?"

My marriage has become something like my churchgoing: a series of formal occasions. We have an equilibrium, and something in me wants to disturb it and something in me wants to keep it.

By the way, I don't expect you to do or say anything about all of this. I want to speak honestly. I want to be as stark and plain as the grass in winter. But at the same time, I hunger for life. I hunger to feel more, to believe more, and I don't know whether to look to the past or the future for this.

Yours,
Veronica

Joe sat with this letter at the kitchen table. The pad of stationery lay in front of him, and he'd already removed his pen from
his pocket and clicked it open. Then closed. Then open again.
He'd written "November 11" and "Dear Veronica." It was dark
early these days, and the evening stretched out long in front of
him. He didn't want her to think she'd offended him with her
frankness. On the contrary, he welcomed it. He wondered how
to match her tone for tone.

There were many things about his life as a priest that pre-
cluded the kind of directness and honesty that Veronica was
offering him. People on the reservation also tended to be direct
in their speech, when they weren't teasing you relentlessly. The
Lakota liked true, raw, unaffected speech, and they also liked
a good joke. You'd think he'd have learned a thing or two from
them. But there was always that veil between him and reservation life. He felt himself obligated to a slightly elevated form of
speech, as if he were about to launch into a homily, and that layered with his natural silence and the burdens of the office meant
that he said less than he meant most of the time.

The voice he'd found to write to Veronica didn't feel practiced
or smooth. It felt more like the jagged edge of a wound. Where
was his qol? What was his connection to that elemental, divine
speech that brought worlds into being? That was too abstract a
question.

He was startled by a knock on the door. When he opened it,
he saw Alice. Her hair was loose and whipping in the raw wind.
The lights of her car behind her on the gravel driveway lit her up
in a kind of glow.

"Bear's gone," she said.

———

Gone. Gone where? Gone how? Where would he go? Bear did not
know the outside world. Except for the occasional shopping trip
to Rapid City, had he ever been anywhere? He was an innocent—

strange to use that word given what he was accused of and given the question of his guilt or innocence. But it was a fact. He was an innocent. A fierce innocent. Now it was winter, so it didn't seem likely that he would be hiding in the woods. The harsh prairie winds tossed the endless grass; snow threatened almost daily and spit occasionally. Already this winter a man had frozen to death walking back to his house from Willie's. You saw people all the time missing fingers and toes from frostbite, from having been caught out in the elements with temperatures dropping and long, empty highways in front of them.

This time they didn't arrange a search party. This time they just waited, feeling Bear's absence like a cold, white island of ice in the creek. The next day Father Joe went into his office and closed the shades to shut out the weak November sun with its rose gold light, and the nubs of the willows that flashed red here and there, and the creek that was slowly turning to ice in thin sheets that grew from the banks toward the center. He needed privacy, even from the creek.

He sat at his desk and dialed the Diocese of Rapid City. He didn't recognize the voice of the woman who answered the phone, which gave him a feeling of relief.

"This is Father Joseph Kreitzer from St. Rose on Windy Creek. How are you this afternoon?" He kept his voice light and friendly. Charming if he could.

"Just fine," she said. She mirrored his tone. "What can I do for you?"

"I am looking for something." He cleared his throat and rubbed his eyes. "I need some school records from the Blessed Sacrament Mission School, and I am wondering where they are kept."

"Blessed Sacrament," the woman said, and paused. "I'm sorry. I don't know where that is. Where in the state are we talking about?"

"It was the mission school here on Windy Creek. Before the

tribe took it over, it was called Blessed Sacrament. Now it's High Horse Indian School. Blessed Sacrament closed about ten years ago. 1973."

Father Joe pictured the woman in front of a memo pad, one of those that had a few lines to take a message. Who called. Time of call. Day of call. Callback number. Perforated edges so that you could tear it out and leave it in the appropriate person's box, but also a carbon copy.

"What kind of records are you looking for?"

Father Joe pressed his fingers to his forehead and tried to remember what Alice had said. "Attendance records. School disciplinary records, that kind of thing."

"I don't know off the top of my head who can help you, Father. Maybe the chancellor's office." Her voice was so mild and easy, so eager to be helpful, Father Joe appreciated it; his own apprehension, the irrational fears that arose in relation to the words "Blessed Sacrament Mission School" didn't seem to bother her one bit. How easily the drama fades once the theater curtains close. How quickly the heat subsides. But somewhere there was a filing cabinet in some basement. They had to find it.

And where was Bear? Alice knew that he felt himself a burden, that he had run with the idea that they would be better off without him. He'd taken his sketchbook with him, and Father Joe took some comfort in that. It meant that he had taken himself with him or perhaps that he had perhaps gone in search something and would return with it, like a prize.

Even as they waited, they had to keep working. Alice had gone to the school office and brought back what she could find there. It wasn't much, which made them both think that the diocese must have taken the bulk of the records with them. Or perhaps destroyed them. That was possible too. But there was now, alongside mimeographed law articles and handwritten notes, a jumble of manila folders and worn plastic sheaths on the kitchen table. She was going through them meticulously, looking for even the slightest clue. She was even looking for what was not said, for slight changes in tone or oblique references—anything that indicated the loss of a student for even a few days or weeks. The past was so fragile. The reality of day-to-day life, even the life that Father Joe and Alice had lived, shared, carried in their own bodies, disappeared from the record of things faster than a breath. How could there be a record there?

Even if you could record it, videotape it with those cameras that people carried around now, it still wouldn't be truth. It would always be partial and broken. Papers were picked out and saved from an immensity of papers. Facts were picked out and saved from an immensity of things that had happened. There didn't seem to be a pattern to this picking and saving. We are chasing a dream, Joe thought. The way a fragment of a dream rises up from some vast ocean, like the flicker of a fish on the water, and as you reach out for it, it's gone. They were looking for a Lakota girl-child. That was not the kind of person records were kept about. How was she going to speak to them amid these jottings that had somehow escaped the trash bin?

When the chancellor called back several days later, he said that the diocese did have some records from the school in the archive, and that there were protocols involved in accessing them. He would send Father Joe the forms, he said, and they could get started on the process.

"Forms?"

"Yes, forms. It will help me a lot to know what you are looking for, and then we'll review them and see what we can do."

"Our situation is quite urgent," Father Joe said. He didn't want to use the word "desperate."

"I understand," the man said. Father Joe doubted it. "Let's just get the i's dotted and the t's crossed. We'll do this one by the book."

By the book. Of course he would. He's got nothing to lose by going by the book.

"He says we'll go by the book and that the process of accessing the files could take weeks or months," he told Alice in part because he knew she would share his irritation. "Who is he protecting anyway? It seems to me that it's a child that is threatened, not an institution. They already lost the school. You'd think they wouldn't have anything left to lose."

"You'd think," Alice said as if she'd only partly heard him.

Father Joe thought of a line from Psalm 50. When God does speak, among the things he says is "I will accept no bull from thy house."

"Alice." Father Joe pulled out one of the worn kitchen chairs, with foam poking through the plastic and a scratched metal frame. He sat down. "They are planning to close St. Rose."

She did not look up from her yellow pad, but she did stop writing.

"How long have we got you for?" she said after a pause.

"Easter," he said. "I bargained for Easter."

Alice glanced at the phone. This was her new habit, to glance at the phone, expecting some news of Bear. That the police had him. That someone on the reservation had talked him into calling. Or that the phone would yield some new clue that would lead them to Bear's mother. It sat on the wall, the long cord twisting to the floor.

"What about you?" she said.

"They say Hastings, Nebraska, but I don't know. I might go to Sioux Falls and feed the homeless or something. Maybe they could find something for me to do there."

She reached her hand across the table, and Father Joe picked it up and held it. He studied her long brown fingers entangled in his hairy knuckles. He didn't look at her, but he felt his throat tighten.

"We are a bulwark, Father," she said. "A bulwark. We will not be shaken."

12

Time on Low Wages

A WIND PICKED UP as November ground on, and it pelted them without the snow that normally accompanied it. It rattled the windows in the rectory and tossed the chairs on Gayle's porch. It blew leaves up against Alice's house and plastic bags into tangled masses among the willows. Dust spun up from the cracked ground and swirled candy wrappers in tiny tornados. "This wind," people took to saying without adding any more to the phrase.

Father Joe pulled up the cellar door in the ferocious wind and climbed down the warped steps into the basement to find the Advent wreath. Father Joe had forgotten how many boxes were down in that space—his own archives. He wondered for a moment if he should start pulling them up. He'd have to go through them anyway before spring, to create his own version of the facts of the Father Kreitzer Era, and all of Alice's questions made him wonder if maybe there was something that they were looking for in them. He couldn't imagine what, but he was learning to lean hard into maybes and vague possibilities.

He climbed back up, closed the inner door, and secured the outer door with a padlock. Back inside the church, he pulled out the purple linens for Advent. He'd told Alice he'd bring them over to her house, where she washed them by hand. Why had he not noticed before how threadbare they were? Rags really. He saw that Alice had layered them—probably for years now—to cover up holes and stains and places where the fabric had started to give way to time and become a see-through grid.

As he carried the linens out to the Buick, he found he was bothered by their raggedness. The last Advent at St. Rose. Why not use the old scraps? That was the logical thing to do, give them one more year and then burn them at Easter in the vigil fire. But that was just it, what bothered Father Joe. They would hand nothing down to the future. St. Rose would wither and disappear as if it had been tumbleweed in the wind, like the old church in White Pine, north of the reservation. He thought about the man who sat on the steps there and called himself Harry Crog. He asked anyone who walked by for money, for a ride, for a cigarette, for a bottle. The church steps were the backdrop for Crog's peculiar theater, but beyond that it was an empty shell of a place.

An idea struck him. Completely impractical given what they were facing. Irrational even, but he couldn't leave it alone. What if Alice beaded a new Advent altar cloth? It would only be used for one season, yes, at least in this space, but it would say something about St. Rose that could live on. It would come from Alice's hands, and it would speak to the future somehow. He imagined it like one of Alice's bright shawls that she beaded for the children before powwows—delicate, tenacious—with a rose at the center. Like Alice, like Jackie. To have something of that in St. Rose during this time of lasts.

He should have thought of this years ago, not going through the motions, year after year, not attending to the wear, the gentle and not-so-gentle, the constant erosion of their life together. To ask now made no sense at all. And yet he imagined helping her, his clumsy fingers learning, at this late stage, to bead. "Ridiculous," said the voice.

Father Joe drove in the thickening dark to Alice's house and pulled up in front. The house was quiet. For a change, there was no one on the porch or in the yard. There was a sense of desertion about the place. The weeds that bent in the wind looked weedier. The paint looked more peeled. The wood looked more battered.

He wondered if the door was open, and he could lay the cloths inside and then go home for dinner. He walked up to the screen door with its thin, warped metal and knocked, even though it was obvious no one was home. When he opened the screen door, a piece of paper fell out. It was folded into many tiny squares, but he recognized it right away as a page from Bear's sketchbook. He picked it up and sat on one of the porch chairs, feeling the wind pierce his inner ear. He looked around. No sign of the boy anywhere, not that he expected Bear to reappear until he was ready to reappear. Father Joe didn't expect to see him by accident as he had the first time.

He sat and held the paper in his hands, and he found himself praying. *Please help him. Whatever he needs. Wherever he is. Please be with him.* He sat for a long time while the wind wailed around him. He listened to the leaves shake from the cottonwoods and felt it all the way through, letting himself long for warmth, long for light.

Eventually, he had no idea how long, he heard tires on gravel and saw the lights from a car turn into the driveway.

When Alice got out, her hair was flying, and for a moment he had the illusion that she might lift off the ground.

"Father," she said. "You're here! I was just at your house looking for you."

"Alice, I . . ."

"I've got our first clue!" she said. "It's not much yet, but it is a little seed. The mustard seed, right?" She smiled.

She was talking while leading them into the house and turning on the lights.

When she turned around to look at him, he held out the paper to her. "This was in the door."

She held it in her palm. "What is it?"

"I don't know. But that's Bear's paper, isn't it?"

She also didn't open it right away. She flew around for a moment. She opened the woodstove and threw some newspaper and some wood inside. She lit a match and watched while the flame caught and spread.

"Okay," she said. The wind in her had quieted a little. She took a deep breath. "Let's have a look."

She unfolded the paper square by square and smoothed it out on the table. Father Joe realized he was hoping for something straightforward, like a letter. "Dear Mom." But what was on the paper was something more mysterious. It was a series of squiggles and symbols. There were stars and feathers and various bird figures. Father Joe felt a wave of annoyance. Did Bear think this was a game? Was he playing? What was he playing at? "Use your words, Bear," he wanted to say, as if Bear were a toddler.

Alice's mouth tightened into a straight line. She didn't say anything as she went into the kitchen and scooped coffee into the percolator, filled the pot with water, and set it on the stove.

"This was in the door?" she said.

"It looks a little like a map maybe," Father Joe said.

"I wonder what he is trying to say."

"It would help if he would use words." There was a growl in Father Joe's voice. Alice ignored it. He took a deep breath.

"He's close by, anyway," she said. "That's something."

"What have you got?"

"I was working through the files, and here's the thing. It looks like in the spring of 1970, the school tried some kind of an attendance program. They were keeping track of who was in class and who wasn't, and they kept the records. Maybe they thought they'd come back to it, but they never did."

"How does this help us?"

"There are names. Names lead to people. The people on the list would have been, what, Albert's age." She paused and they both remembered that if Albert were alive, they could start with him. But then if Albert were alive, there would have been no Vincent in their midst. They wouldn't be searching.

"This is where I am going to start," she said. "Marlena's coming over in a bit with the kids." She got up and pulled a pot from the refrigerator. She put it on the stove and lit a fire under it.

Father Joe rubbed his eyes and then tore a piece of paper from one of the legal pads. He oriented the map and started to copy it, as best he could, including the markings. He worried as he copied that his eyes might miss the most salient details. It was complex and detailed and obtuse.

"Alice," he said while she went to look for potatoes. He watched her movements, so swift and practiced. From above the stove, she took a jar with dried green leaves in it and sprinkled that in the pot. "I brought the linens from the church. But."

She looked up.

"But they are so sad-looking. I had this idea. I don't know what you'll think." Father Joe realized he was having trouble saying what had been so clear in his mind only hours before. "I should have thought of it ages ago."

"Say it, Father. Use your words."

He blushed and looked up at her. "I think we should have a new altar cloth for Advent, and I think it should be beaded." He paused. "By you. And I could help. I know it doesn't make any sense, but I want to."

She was chopping potatoes and a carrot next to the stove. "Something of St. Rose to go on," she said. She knew his mind. She knew how he moved and how he thought.

"Yes." He was quiet.

"Let's see about it, then," she said. "Maybe I can do it at night since I'm not sleeping anyway."

"I can join you," he said. "A vigil."

Alice called Father Joe the next morning to report that she had awakened to a fresh stack of firewood next to the shed. She had not heard it arrive. "And you know it's not because I was sleeping well. I was up half the night staring at the moon."

They both then thought of Bear's upcoming court appearance. If he would only come to them by then, they could keep buying a little time with their low wages.

13

No Snow

Dear Veronica,

If only it would snow. The ground is frozen. The creek is frozen. But still no snow. I've been occasionally translating, as I mentioned, although things have taken a difficult turn here, and I've not been at it much. If I keep on at this rate, God will have to keep me alive like Jehoiada to finish the psalms.

Joe was writing at the kitchen table. In all the rectory, that felt like the right place to meet Veronica. A somewhat rickety chair that squeaked when he rocked on it, the last of the coffee in the drip pot. The plain pad of stationery. Silence. The kitchen light overhead too bright and glaring, but he did not feel like changing it. He'd smoothed out Veronica's letter next to him, with the soft loops of her handwriting in blue pen on a higher quality of paper than his own.

I don't love Psalm 50, truth be told. It's harsh and in some moods, I read it and it sounds greedy and off-putting, hard-hearted; God uses His voice to testify against His people, which I mean, granted, they generally deserve. But it doesn't make for comforting reading.

But in other moods, I can hear God saying, "I know every creature of the earth—every vole in Veronica Foster's meadow in Harrisburg, South Dakota. Every chickadee and every sparrow." I try then to imagine that kind of knowledge, vast and intimate at the same time.

I find verse 12 quite mysterious. "If I were hungry, I should not tell you." Every time I read that line, I think, "Why not?" Why would God keep His hungers from us? What would it mean to serve a hungry God, one who made His needs known? But then I picture all the old men trying to feed a hungry God with their sacrifices—their meat and their blood. And I think, "Yes there is wisdom in God keeping His hungers from us, after all." Maybe God is saying, "I don't eat meat; I eat love." He would gladly eat gratitude, He says. He would gladly eat kept promises.

In your letter, you also mention hunger. Like you, I wonder what we do with our hungers at this moment in our lives. The bishop says that he is moving me to a new parish and closing St. Rose. So I will be back in the real world before too long. On the rez, as they say, you have to take hunger literally. Since Reagan closed the Office of Economic Opportunity a couple of years ago, the people are often hungry. Well, I mean, they've long been. We've tried to fill in with a food pantry and some commodity sharing. I'm guessing you may have never seen a box of that waxy government cheese, have you? Apparently they've got that stocked up in abundance. When it gets here, it's moldy.

But I imagine out there, hunger is a different thing, fed by a thousand whims. I wonder how I will live in that world.

Meanwhile, if only it would snow.

In peace,
Joseph

Alice had begun her beading project the night before Bear's check-in with the tribal court. He had not made an appearance, but Alice had calmed since he had made his presence, close at hand, known. She thought he was up to something important, and when he came back, it would be to good ends. Father Joe didn't feel that same confidence. He wanted clarity. He wanted the symbols on Bear's map to correspond to direct clues, like a treasure hunt.

He knocked on her door on the evening before the hearing. She had laid out the beads in purples, blues, and whites and sketched a rose on the cloth for the center, and then patterns emanating out from the rose in triangles. Alice showed him how to attach the beads with tiny tucks of the thread, but then she looked at his fingers and said, "You know, Father Joe, those don't look like beading fingers to me." He looked at his hands: the wide knuckles, the beefy tips, hair sprouting in random directions.

"Why don't you just hand them to me as I go?" Her hands flew with amazing swiftness, aligning and attaching the beads to the piece of cloth that she had made her sketches on. They worked in a silent rhythm, every once in a while hearing the wind shake the house.

"Father," she said as they slowed in their work. "We are going to have to face them tomorrow without Bear."

"Have you called the lawyer?" Father Joe asked. She shook her head.

"He will say we are going to lose Bear."

"Yes," he said.

"Did I ever tell you about when I was a little girl and they sent me to boarding school?"

"Only a little," he said.

"Those worlds. They were so different." She straightened her shoulders and held the needle up. "I was only six years old. After I was born, they sterilized my mother. Did I ever tell you that?

They were trying to make the Indian problem go away by making sure there were no more Indians. In a generation, we'd be gone. That was the plan at the boarding school: make us something other than Indian. Make us white. For speaking Indian, you could get beaten. But a lot of us didn't know the old language anyway, because our mothers and grandmothers thought things would go better for us if we didn't know.

"They tried killing us out of existence. Then they tried starving us. Freezing us. Diseasing us. Then they tried educating us out of existence.

"Do you know why that failed, Father? Why we're still here?"

"I don't," he admitted. "I've always thought of the Sioux as strong." The words felt somehow less than what he wanted to say.

She shook her head. "You do know what Sioux means, right? It's not our word. It means 'little snakes.'" She paused to let him take in that information. "But for us, we know we are here because of the land. That's what called us. That's what saved us. The land needs us and so it didn't let us go."

Father Joe didn't know whether to look at her, with her eyes by turns dark and light, or to look at the floorboards or study the peeling linoleum of the tabletop.

"Our way of life is rooted in the land. The land first. The land always. We are the land. The land is us. So long as the land endures, we endure. And maybe, maybe our way, which is the stronger, will win out, and everyone will know it and will live by the way of the land."

They lapsed into silence. Father Joe pictured the woods behind Ghost Lake, the lonely road up to Gayle's house, the arrowheads hiding in places only Bear knew.

"We should go to bed," he said at last. "We don't want to start any rumors."

She grinned. "I'll see you in the morning."

In the morning, the sky was clear, with streaks of lavender, purple, rose, and gray. In the early dawn, Father Joe made coffee and sat down at the Formica-topped table while it percolated. He set out the rough sketch of Bear's map in front of him and stared at it. He ran his finger along the central line.

What was Bear up to? What was he doing out there, wherever he was? What did this note have to do with it?

Suddenly he knew what he had to do. He knew exactly where to go with a certainty that belied the jumble of images on the page. He would go early, before Alice would have to call the lawyer, before the meeting with the judge and the probation officer. He took three gulps of his coffee and then put on his collar and his coat.

The driveway was icy, and he moved carefully. He felt himself on guard, but then he saw his careful step as something more than the conditions of the morning. Ever since Rossling had dismissed him, he'd been afraid of the letter that might come in the mail or a reprimand that might end up in a file somewhere with his name on it. He'd moved like this—shuffling on ice so as not to fall. He had not wanted to disturb the hierarchy. That innate caution had not served him well, he thought as he moved to the car and dug the scraper out of the back seat.

He started the Buick to get it warming and then scraped raggedly at the ice on the windshield until it was clear enough that he could see through. It's not that I want to become incautious, he said to no one through the frost of the morning into the soft light of dawn. You have to have some caution when you are dealing with these people. Who did he mean by "these people"? He supposed he meant the bishop. He meant his reassignment. He meant his future. But who would his caution serve at the end of the day? It felt like they had all always been saying "Be careful."

Rossling and Fabian. The whole priesthood felt itself threatened at every turn. It had to be guarded, and they needed men like Father Joe to participate in the guarding. Father Joe had obeyed. And now, he asked, to what end?

Obedience. Now there was a question worth pondering.

He drove off the highway onto the packed, ice-rimmed dirt of Gayle's road and up toward the trailer. He opened the screen door and paused before knocking. Beyond the thin door, he heard voices. Gayle's deep and resonant; Bear's fainter but distinct. He couldn't make out the words. He paused. Should he go in? Should he remain outside? By now, they knew he was there. There was no hiding the drive up the hill and the revving noise of the Buick's engine.

He pushed open the door. Inside he saw Gayle hunched in front of the woodstove, poking at some embers with a stick. He didn't turn, although Father Joe knew he knew he was there. Bear was gone. Gayle added a log to the embers and then said. "Good morning, hoksila. You are early. Or late. I guess I don't know which." He chuckled.

When the fire was going strong and its crackling filled the room, he turned and stood up. He was a tall man, well over six feet.

"Wakalapi ya cin ho?" he asked. He walked toward the kitchen. "It's not that cat-piss coffee that you drink. I've got the good stuff."

"Bear's here."

He grunted what sounded like an affirmative.

Father Joe shoved his hands into the pockets of his pants and rocked back and forth on his heels. "He's got a check-in with the courts today. If he misses that appointment . . ."

There was another grunt as Gayle filled the percolator with water and added coffee and then set the pot on the woodstove.

He gestured to a chair, and Father Joe sat. The logs settled and sighed. The pipe from the stove creaked as it expanded.

A white light had started to filter into the room through the small windows of the trailer.

"The boy is working some things out," he said finally. "He needs time."

"We don't have it."

Gayle lifted his eyebrows and nodded. He looked down at the rough floorboards. "He's reckoning," he said at last. "When he's done reckoning, he'll come back. That's all I can say."

"Could you at least tell him, remind him, about the meeting today?"

He rose and opened the woodstove door. He poked at the logs there, which muttered reassuringly, as if in response.

14

Mission

FATHER JOE DROVE straight to the church and opened the door for mass. He had only a few minutes to pull things together for whatever small crowd gathered. His hands shook as he vested for the last week before Advent. Should he tell Alice what he knew? Should he keep it to himself? He tried to imagine himself as calm and expert as Gayle making the coffee. He tried to imagine his hands as graceful as the old man's as he laid out the paten and put a few wafers on it and filled the cruets with wine and water.

Alice came in boots and her parka. When Joe saw her, he felt a sharp pain in his chest. She looked more fragile and more undaunted than ever. Her deep cheekbones, the lines on her face. She carried the weight of all of them; he wondered how it didn't crush her. She walked as though unafraid, but he noticed a slight slump now in her shoulders and wondered how long it had been there.

She was here, he supposed, looking for courage to face the day, to face whatever judgment lay in it.

"The Lord be with you," he said.

"And with your spirit," the few murmured.

"What is it, Father?" Alice said at the door.

"I'm going with you today," he said. "Whatever it is, let's do it together."

She nodded simply and turned her face away. "I would like to sleep again," she said. "Like I did when the kids were little. I would go around the house and touch each one on the head, like a blessing, and then lay down and sleep like the dead. No dreams or anything."

Throughout the morning, the clouds to the west built a great gray tower that suggested snow. "I'm liking the look of those," Father Joe said to Alice as they walked toward the tribal court building. "It could snow."

"We're just going to tell the truth," she said. "We're not going to make any excuses. No apologies. This is what happened, and that's it."

When they got to the door of the probation officer's office, the door was locked. A piece of torn notebook paper was taped to the door with a note in blue marker. "Conference call until noon."

"They might've let us know," Father Joe said, annoyed.

"Maybe it's lucky," Alice said. "You can never have too few meetings with these people."

They sat for a moment on the plastic chairs like schoolchildren outside the principal's office. Then Alice said, "This is a dark path. I keep wondering where the light is going to come from. I keep thinking: it's going to come from Bear knowing who he is. I don't mean like they mean—" She gestured at the door and its hastily scribbled note. "Whether he's an Indian or he's not an Indian. I mean, will he know who he is, his place in the world, how much he matters? Sometimes it seems to me that the only thing that matters from all of this is if he learns that."

She waited a moment, as if for Father Joe to find some words to reassure her. When he didn't, she said, "Let's go to my house. I want to show you something."

Father Joe had a feeling of anticlimax, prepared as he had thought he had been to face down the bureaucracy. They drove in tandem back to Alice's house. Ahead of him, Father Joe watched the Volare swerve on the icy road. Not exactly a winter-worthy vehicle. But that's how it was out here. You didn't try to get the right tool for the job. You made the best of what you had. Alice had a genius for that.

They probably didn't let him drive the Buick in Hastings. In a place like that, you had to keep your image up. You had to present well. The church was probably eighty percent image and twenty percent ritual. Here image was pretty worthless. Lydia tried to keep up with it. She thought there was value in present-ing well. But no one else had the energy for it, with the poverty and the endless grinding down. Joblessness. Homelessness. Drunken fools. Hungry children. The hopeless were visible. If Alice was right, then the ones with hope stayed out of sight. They stayed far on the edges of things, tending to the remnants of ways that Father Joe knew nothing about. Or maybe they'd been in plain sight, right in front of his face the whole time, and he wouldn't know it.

When he thought of going to a place where everyone had ex-actly what they needed—shiny new tools, shiny new sanctuar-ies, where he understood everything because everything was exactly as they said it would be—that thought was depressing. What good was his life if he understood things? Or maybe he would get there and see, for the first time, that he didn't under-stand those good midwestern people at all and never had. That these people here on Windy Creek, with their secrets and their wounds, were all he would ever understand. The kind of loneli-ness he had cultivated here would not serve him well out there.

Alice had a list of five names that she'd gleaned from the

attendance records. The plan was to take them to the county courthouse in Hanson and see if she could look up anything more.

"Police records, truancy, public drunkenness. Something that tells us about a desperate girl. We've got to try to imagine ourselves into her skin. What would cause you to abandon your just-born child to strangers? Could be an abusive parent, an abusive boyfriend, could be she was homeless, nowhere to go. Could be she wanted to go to the bar and get drunk. Desperate people sometimes leave marks that people who aren't desperate don't."

Father Joe looked out the window. The sky had softened into gray. The sun had disappeared. The first flakes of snow were falling on the hardened ground.

"I said we were strangers to her," Alice went on. "But what if we weren't strangers. She trusted you when she didn't trust the people at the school, and people around here don't go around trusting priests. I wonder if she knew you or thought she knew you."

"Knew me?"

"Do you keep those books that we have at the back of the church, where people sign in if they are visiting? What if she signed in? In that perfect handwriting. Maybe she would have wanted to leave a record of herself in the place where she left her child."

"I think that's a long shot."

"It's all long shots now. Where are the books?"

"I think they are in the basement, but I just can't think they'd be meaningful."

"Just look, Father."

He didn't tell her about Bear. If he told her, she'd drive out there, and Gayle had said Bear needed time. The probation officer was somehow preoccupied and now there was a storm coming. If he was reading the sky right, they were in for a long one. He pictured the roads in and out of the reservation blocked, businesses and government offices shut down. Schools closed. What he felt in that was time.

Back at the church, he found the key for the padlock. When he opened the cellar door, he saw an ice floe that turned the steps into a hazard. It ran all the way down the warped stairs like a tiny river and then under the door. It occurred to him that if he fell and broke an ankle, no one would find him there for a good long time. He imagined himself crumpled at the bottom of the stairs, calling out a pathetic "help" and no one within hearing distance.

He'd seen the boxes when he'd gone down to the basement for the Advent wreath. They sat in hulking impotence in one corner, waiting for the dumpster or for a fire. It was so rare that someone signed one of those books. There weren't going to be many of them amid the old hymnals and the stacks of papers he'd never taken the time to sort and had piled up in an office cleaning frenzy one day who knew how many years ago. Would there be a record of St. Rose somewhere, someday? An archive? A drawer in a filing cabinet? Would a historian a hundred years hence want to poke around in St. Rose's records looking for evidence of something? Would someone be inclined to write a history of this place that was, in fact, no place—a far-flung, weedy patch of mission?

"Mission." That was the word that was supposed to have filled Father Joe with inspiration. That was the old-world word they had used in the *Midwest Catholic Reporter*. It had been intended to make Father Joe sound brave, a frontiersmen, going out into the wilds, where few were willing to go. It was intended to make the Lakota people sound wild and savage. It conjured the priests of old who carried the church on their backs into the wilderness in their black robes and early deaths from dysentery. All of that was still hidden in the word.

And then there was the town of Mission: a devastated place. Hollow. Father Joe had been there once or twice, and it never failed to fill him with cynicism. He made sure not to stay until after dark when things got chaotic and violent, and people spilled out of the bar with all that pent-up rage that life on and around the reservation could bring you. The people had this look in their eyes—white and Indian—that said "I have nothing to lose." There was a mission there, but you would need to be some kind of saint to find it. Typically, if Father Joe had a choice, he drove around Mission, not through it.

But despite all of that, he thought he might still believe in mission, after all, but maybe not in the way other people meant. What he might believe in were the cycles of their life at St. Rose. The day-in, day-out rituals, invisible to anyone outside the church but at the same time a part of the whole globe. The way that one season gave way to the next, and Year A gave way to Year B and so on. Like Alice's beads, each one connected to the next in a vivid pattern. Living a life based on those circles of season and scripture and year—that's what had connected him. Now that they were living their last cycle, he knew that theoretically he could join that ritual anywhere in the world. They would say the same things in Hastings, Nebraska, or in Nairobi. They would say them in Washington, DC, or Nicaragua. Likewise, the people of St. Rose could simply move on and say and do it all at Blessed Sacrament. It's all the same, anywhere. That was the point of mission. To make it all the same everywhere, even to the ends of the earth.

The *Midwest Catholic Reporter* celebrated his role in making it the same. Even to Windy Creek, they might say, the gospel had been carried, even to those people who so obviously needed it and yet who resisted it. Even there the Word of the Lord is declared. But that was the part that he felt slipping away from him now, as it was coming to an end. St. Rose was particular.

Even peculiar. An outlier, an anomaly. A very particular kind of no place.

It's no wonder the old men in black figured they could wipe it off the map with a simple administrative sweep of the hand. It didn't fit. For a moment, he imagined telling them that he would continue, without pay, in the little building under which he now stood. "Just carry me out when I'm dead, and then you can have your consolation." But a thousand objections appeared in his mind with that thought. The rectory—who would pay the heating bill? The car. They'd take it back. Lydia—no one would pay her either. Could he live on hard tack and sleep on a cot next to the furnace like one of the mission priests from the stories? Maybe Gayle would take him in.

"The Tale of Father Joseph Kreitzer: From Mission Priest to Charity Case." People would say he took to drinking. They would talk.

Under the naked bulb of the basement light, he identified the boxes in question. The ice floe had tacked some of them to the floor, likely warped the contents. The first box contained old bulletins and devotional guides, all dated to the late '70s. Another was full of hymnals. A third contained a more miscellaneous collection that he thought might have promise. There were parish ledgers inside, with baptismal, marriage, and death records, so maybe there were also guest books. His eye caught on something else: papers, rolled scroll-like and held together with a now tatty rubber band. When he picked the bundle up, the rubber band immediately broke and left a sticky residue on his fingers. It felt strangely to him like an invitation, like the papers were inviting themselves to be read. It took him a moment to remember what they were.

The one on top, in slightly smudged blue mimeographed ink, began,

High Horse, South Dakota 57572

October 20, 1969

Dear Bishop Carson,

Many a moon has passed since I've written to you, and I do apologize. August was busy trying to get teachers. Just as we thought we had the school year all lined up, one sister left and another was recalled. Getting school underway was a real challenge. The lay council made an all-out effort to round up dropouts and got a number of them back in school. We've got 473 children enrolled, and about 200 or even less are boarders, a drop from last year.

We seem to be quite fortunate in having a good religious and lay faculty. We had to let our coach go. You may remember him, Robert Conlin. He really wouldn't do his job. We had a few incidents I won't go into. There's more than a bit of a drinking problem. So we do need a coach and a librarian to fill out our team.

———

The voice was unmistakable to him. He didn't need to see the signature at the bottom. Fabian. Fabian who appeared in his dreams, standing by doorways as if waiting for Father Joe to leave or sitting on a leather chair with a pipe, appearing and disappearing as an apparition. In those days, the bishop was an affable, detached man working to make his Rapid City diocese as much like suburban Minneapolis as he possibly could. He asked for quarterly letters from all of them. He liked the letters to be chatty, if possible. A bit of gossip would make him feel like he was getting the real story. Fabian excelled at the form. Look at how he said nothing. The bishop would hear himself praised for how well he provided for the poor school and the needs of the poor children. Fabian also managed to praise himself, demonstrating how good he was at overcoming obstacles. But then he sprinkled in the drunkenness of one of the coaches, making sure to let the bishop know he had the problem under control. The underlying message was that the man was one of the lay staff, of course, as if those problems existed only among the unwashed. The letter didn't mention Brother Chapman, whom Father Joe knew for a fact had been drinking himself silly every night in this same period.

Father Joe had forgotten that he had these letters, a convenient sort of forgetting. Repression, he thought, is what the Freudians would call it. Obtaining these letters had been perhaps the most awkward thing Father Joe had ever done. The secretary at Blessed Sacrament Mission School had given them to him on a brief and highly secretive loan when Father Joe had decided that if no one else would get rid of Flynn, he would do it himself. He'd hastily photocopied them on a bright afternoon in October of 1972.

The whole reservation had been in a kind of chaos during those days. Everyone was watching nervously for news of the happenings on Pine Ridge, where Dick Wilson had been elected tribal chairman and American Indian movement was marching on Washington. It was astonishing how they could be only a few miles away and get so little news of it. News, no. Rumors, yes. Bank robberies, prison storming, plans to set the state capital on fire. The *Rapid City Journal* and the *Sioux Falls Argus Leader* didn't deliver to Windy Creek, so Father Joe would go over to Blessed Sacrament to scan for news because the secretary would bring the papers into the school from Wagner. The government might send in federal troops. People were turning up dead. Most of the talk was obscured from Father Joe—who would want to fill him in? What would he ask if he did find a willing informant? The newspapers were vague. They reported on the housing that Wilson wanted to build and advertised for construction workers, when Father Joe knew for a fact all hell was breaking loose over there. It was hard to tell if they actually had anyone reporting from Pine Ridge at all.

The last straw with Flynn had been a few weeks earlier when a young woman, the daughter of an older member of St. Rose—a pious woman who came to mass every morning and the Wednesday afternoon rosary group, who brought canned goods to the food pantry and had asked him to bless a picture she had found at the Wagner thrift store of the sacred heart of Jesus—had come to see him.

The younger woman sat in his office on the threadbare couch, looking down. She held her arms protectively in front of her chest, like she thought Father Joe might attack. They sat in silence while he waited for her to speak her business and she stared at the floorboards.

"My mom said I should come to you," she said finally. "My mom said you are a good man and you would know what to do."

Father Joe shifted self-consciously in his chair.

"I got a little boy who is starting over at Blessed Sacrament. He's only five, Father. My mother says it's the right place for him. She says we're Catholics and that's the Catholic school. She went there, and I went there, and she says that's the place for us."

Father Joe cleared his throat, although he wasn't sure if there was something to say. A long silence followed while the young woman seemed to be waiting for something, with her long hair falling in front of her face and her crossed leg moving back and forth rapidly, her foot jumping like a fish on a line.

"Is there a problem?" he said finally.

She did not look up. "I want something better for him, Father, than what I got. And that place."

Father Joe stared at her dark, bent head and considered the courage it took this young woman to say what she had said to a priest. He'd heard stories, going back decades, about the Sisters of the Sacred Heart, about small rooms in the attic where children were sent for punishment and beatings that took place regularly.

But in the silence, the woman seemed to be saying something else, and it was like listening through a door that was closed, muffled sounds only from which he was left to make meaning. He wanted to hear her, but so much stood between them.

She must've decided that she had said what she came to say. He'd offered her nothing, but he had let the question stay between them without refutation. She stood. He also stood.

"I will look into things," he said, and felt almost crippled by the voice that now said, "Ridiculous."

He walked her to the front door and touched her shoulder. She turned half toward him and then turned away. When she was gone, and he had sat back down in his office, he thought, *Flynn. At the very least, I will see to it that Flynn goes.*

Fabian would be of no help. Anything that he did to approach Fabian about this was a dead end. Fabian's officiousness, his defensiveness, his cool demeanor would make a mockery of Joe's attempts. And the divide between the priests and the Indians was growing. He felt it every day. The priests started many conversations with "If it weren't for us . . ." as if the thing that was missing was gratitude.

Meanwhile, the atmosphere was stirring with something new. A new naming. The smell of smoke from a prairie fire, far off but distinctive. It was violent and threatened violence. Dangerous. It went against all of Father Joe's instincts and filled him with a sense of dread. The voice in his head said, "Whose side are you on, Joe?" And sometimes it felt like that voice was coming from Fabian or from the bishop, and other times it felt like the voice was coming from Alice. But when had there become sides? he wondered. He had lived here for more than a decade without sides. He was a people's priest. A servant of both the church and the people. Weren't they one and the same? He felt naive when he asked that question.

And so he decided to get the files. If he could find one word about Flynn, he would write to the archdiocese. He would go over

Fabian's head and tell the archbishop about these illicit trades that tossed men like Flynn onto the reservation. He would point out how badly that hurt relations. They should know that this was happening right under their noses.

He knew the secretary was on his side. She had rolled her eyes with him at the same antics among the staff. She let him sit behind the counter to read the newspapers and brought him coffee in a Styrofoam cup. They'd exchanged opinions under their breath about interdepartmental politics and official statements of harmony. She knew about the all-too-common drinking problems. Father Joe was kept apart as a parish priest, and Debra was kept apart because she was a laywoman—an outsider to the religious establishment and an outsider to the reservation. So she and Joe exchanged sympathies.

Still it was a risk. If she breathed one word of this to Fabian or to anyone . . .

He'd driven over to the school that day on the icy morning roads with a churn in his belly that he knew was fear, and he shamed himself for it. "Coward," said the voice. What a companion shame was. What a constant presence. It was like a policeman inside his head, always telling him where the boundary was. How often he turned toward it to hear its icy pronouncements.

He'd parked in the parking lot under the oaks. No one would be surprised to see his car there. He noted the sound of his loafers on the sidewalk, the school at a slight distance, the long flight of steps up to the front door. He entered through the heavy doors: the office on the right when you walked in, the smell of furniture polish, the gleam of the floors that he knew the students cleaned.

Debra was at her desk. Students were in class. Fabian was . . . where? Father Joe tried to imagine his daily routine.

"Here are the newspapers for you, Father," Debra said, laying them on the counter between them.

"I'm working on a brief history of St. Rose," he said a little too quickly, noticing his racing heart, feeling the veins bulge in his neck. "Especially its connection to Blessed Sacrament." He cleared his throat and shoved his hands deep into his pockets. He rocked back and forth on his heels and jiggled the change in his pockets. "I was thinking it might be helpful to have Father Fabian's quarterly letters. You know, it's a good record of the place. I'd just like to run some copies to jog my memory. You understand."

She looked at him carefully, her hands folded in front of her on the surface of polished wood. He could only imagine that she was thinking of the thinness of his pretext. The request was out of the ordinary, but he knew that she was not in the habit of saying no to priests.

"I have them here," she said carefully. She went over to a locked filing cabinet, took a ring of keys from the belt loop of her twill skirt, and opened the drawer.

"I'd feel better," she said with an affected mildness as she handed him a manila folder, "if you might photocopy them someplace else, and then return them here right away."

"You betcha," Father Joe said, matching her mildness, and smiled, even though he could feel redness spreading across his cheeks and blotching his neck.

He had driven to Pierre under the bright October sky with the scrub oak reddening and the grasses undulating silver and green in the wind. "Whose side are you on, Joe?" The Buick almost sighed with pleasure when it turned off Windy Creek's dirt roads and onto the highway.

He'd returned the file in perfect condition before lunch, and he watched as Debra put it directly back into the file cabinet without looking at him. It was as if, in his absence, shame had overtaken her, and she was not going to acknowledge what had just happened. She did not look at him as the drawer closed with a solid smack and she turned the key.

15

Dynamics of Freedom

THE PERHAPS still more humiliating truth for Father Joe as he climbed out of the basement a decade after these events, maneuvering the icy stairs and shutting the cellar door in the whirling snow, was that he had never even read those letters. He'd spent nearly two weeks arguing with himself about them, about his integrity and his judgment, with the intensity of his shame and the betrayal that he now represented to himself and to everyone. And then he hadn't read them. They'd sat like doomsday in a drawer in his office, and he'd managed to pretend that he had much business elsewhere. At the end of October, the news came that the church had worked out an agreement with the tribe. The school would come under the control of the tribal council with a committee of parents and grandparents and community members. They would make the transition quickly, opening the school under new leadership with the name High Horse Indian School after the first of the year. Fabian to Oregon. Flynn would disappear again.

So Father Joe had rolled up his betrayal into a bundle and carried it down to the basement buried in a box of office odds and ends.

Even now, having found them and having broken their rubber band like an invitation to a party he didn't want to attend, he did not read them. He put the box in the back seat of the car. A decade ago, he had told himself daily that if he waited long enough and said nothing, problems would solve themselves. Now he knew that was not true, but he felt that old procrastination rise in steely cold from his abdomen. He would read them, he said to himself. For Bear. For Alice.

At the same time, the whole thing could wait until he got back from the post office. With this storm, he might not be able to go to the post office again for days.

The roads were growing icy and slick, with snow accumulating quickly and cars leaving tracks that were quickly covered with new snow. He greeted Jolene, waved at Jeremy, and took his stack of mail from the post office box. There was, and he now knew he'd been hoping for it, a letter from Veronica.

He drove back to the church, feeling his tires sway on the road, the sky already dimming, darker because of the dense clouds and heavy snow but also because of the November gloom. He decided to read the letter in the car, before getting out, before going back to his office. He sat on the blue velour of the Buick with the engine off, hearing the snow fall on the windshield in tiny splats. Inside the envelope, there was only one thin sheet of paper with the loops of her handwriting, grown larger in some kind of haste.

Dear Joseph,

I am imagining that I might get in the car right now, while the roads are still dry, and drive all the way to the Black Hills. We stayed once at the Sylvan Lake Resort. It's probably closed in the winter, isn't it, when the tourists go back to wherever they came from? But I could get a room somewhere, at some roadside motel. Or some friends of ours have a cabin near Spearfish, and the key is under the mat.

The idea would be just to drive. To drive and to meet you somewhere, a diner, a place that doesn't even have a name where they serve chicken-fried steak and iceberg lettuce salads. I want to put this restlessness on the road somehow. Do you have any idea what I mean, or does it sound like pure insanity to you?

I'm about halfway through Maritain's Scholasticism and Politics, and I am struggling with what he means by the freedom of spontaneity, but I think I could probably demonstrate it by getting in the car right now, couldn't I? And perhaps by the time I reach our NoName Diner in NoName, South Dakota, I will be able to explain it to you perfectly because I wouldn't have just thought about it. I would have lived it, if only for a moment.

But, in truth, I imagine I am here for the duration. I wouldn't want to go off the road at Kadoka and freeze to death before the highway patrol got to me.

Yours,
Veronica

In the car, Father Joe slowly, silently folded the letter and placed it back in the envelope. He felt as if her restlessness had reached through the handwriting, through the paper, into his body and had taken over. He leaned a hot cheek against the cold window and softly tapped the envelope against his knee.

Then he opened the door, setting his black shoes on the blanket of unmarked white, and took the box from the back seat. At the door of the church, he set the box down on the snow, unlocked the church with Veronica's letter between his teeth, and went inside.

He was arrested by the smell of candle wax and linseed oil, the familiar clarifying smell that had told him who he was for so long.

At his desk, he reached into the box and picked up one of the guest books with a puffy brown cover and gold embossment. What a strange thing, people writing their names here the way people leave marks on trees or graffiti on walls. What a strange and universal need: to leave a mark on the world, to assert one's existence against an indifferent backdrop. Each name in the book felt like a small plea, "See me. Remember me. I was here, and I want to matter." He scanned the book page by page for the handwriting of the perfect B. Visitors were not all that common at St. Rose, but when they came, they came from all over: Mobridge, Plankinton, Sioux Falls, Winner, Mission. Most of these towns were as desolate as Windy Creek itself. Clapboard houses, tar paper roofs, dwellings slapped together with anything anyone could find, using rotting truck interiors or storage crates or aluminum sheeting to tack on a bedroom when children were born. The happiest people lived the farthest from these far-flung centers in old shacks, out in the wind, where they could watch the elk graze when they came down from the hills in the winter in search of food. The unhappiest spilled out of ramshackle canvas and tarp, screaming at each other at the top of their lungs and fighting about nothing out of the pure need to feel something, to rage against loss and abandonment. In this snowstorm, right now, Father Joe could guarantee it, someone was already falling down, sure to freeze to death during the cold night to come.

He saw many Bs, but no evidence of the perfect B. But he also didn't feel as secure in his judgment as Alice might if she looked it over, so he decided to do an initial scan and set things aside for her in case her eye would be sharper than his. He scanned several books like this while the day outside disappeared. Then he gathered them up and tromped home through the snow. By the time he arrived, his socks and the bottom hem of his pants were soaked.

Dear Veronica,

I will meet you at the NoName Diner in NoName, South Dakota. I'll order the #3—whatever it is. Give me a day and a time. And then I might keep driving west and farther west. Maybe I will get all the way to the ocean and rent a cabin there. That will be my hermitage. You are welcome to visit me

----

He crumpled this letter and tried to hit the wastebasket with a throw. He hit the rim and the paper skittered across the kitchen floor. He took another piece of paper and tried again.

Dear Veronica,

It was lovely to hear

He stared at this line for several minutes. Then he tore this sheet out and aimed again toward the wastebasket. This one bounced in.

Dear Veronica,

Dear Veronica. How can I tell you who I am? If you saw me for who I am, all of your images of the noble priest who serves the poor would disappear in an instant. What would be left? Since the snow is at last falling, and no one will be coming this way for hours, let me catalog for you my failures. I serve a church that is about to abandon me and the people that I have given the best of my life to. But even so, I am meant to be its servant, even as it abandons me. And I might deserve its dismissal. For a decade I've lived my vocation like a man sleepwalking. While the reservation woke up, I fell asleep. I am not much of a brother to the priesthood or much of a father to the Indians. I am unreliable. But my betrayals continue; they continue beyond my will and beyond reason. I know where Alice's son is and I have not told her. She loses sleep. She doesn't eat. She grows gaunt with worry. And still, I am so accustomed to keeping secrets, it is such an old and ingrained habit, that I do it anyway. Even if it means betraying my friends. Even if it means letting my enemies go about their work in the world unmolested. I keep secrets even when my vows don't require it, because that's easier than figuring out right from wrong, dissecting the spoken from the unspoken.

But you don't know who Alice is, do you? I remember now that I have not told you anything about my life.

He stood up and left the letter on the table. He put on his coat, the thickest, warmest one with the fur-lined hood. He dug in the closet next to the door for his snow boots. Then he looked around and saw the letter sitting there, open, naked on the table. So he went to the table and closed the cover of the stationery. That still didn't feel like enough. He put it in the drawer next to the sink.

The drive over to Alice's was treacherous and long. Father Joe drove with the wipers whooshing against the windshield as fast as they could go at five miles an hour, testing his brakes against the ice gently before intersections, hoping not to see any headlights on the road besides his own. He hunched over the steering wheel, knuckles white. When he got to Alice's house, he left the car on the road, not daring the driveway. At the door, he knocked and hesitated only a moment before he pushed open the door. Alice and Bear sat together at the kitchen table. They looked up in surprise at his snowy entrance, as if he were some wild animal seeking shelter.

16

Walking Woman

ONCE BEAR HAD TAKEN Father Joe in, his face turned from surprise to something almost like defiance. Father Joe shook the snow off of his coat and stomped his boots a couple of times on the small rug in front of the door. He shrugged his gloves into the pockets of the coat, but then left the coat and boots on, as if he planned to stay only a minute, and stood awkwardly on the rug, dripping.

"Come in, Father," Alice said. She looked quite serious, and he felt something between them, an obstacle that had emerged with Bear's presence. Whatever Bear and Alice had been talking about before he came in hung in the air, thick and unmistakable, like woodsmoke stinging their eyes. Whatever it was felt strong enough that he couldn't move toward the table, toward them, and join the circle of light over the kitchen table. Despite Alice's invitation he stayed in the shadows by the door.

"Bear's home," Alice said. "He has news."

Father Joe sank into an old armchair near the door and leaned forward with his palms on his knees.

"News?" he said.

Bear looked steadily at Alice, as if she were a conduit or a guide. She turned toward him and nodded.

The boy spoke, looking at the floor but finding his voice nonetheless.

"When I was at Gayle's," he said. "I was asking. I was asking and asking. I didn't even know how to ask, but I knew I had to because I didn't know what to do." He paused and withdrew into his chair a little.

"He had a dream," Alice prompted.

"Two dreams," he said. "My mother is on a road somewhere. She is walking. She is alone."

"A road, huh?" Father Joe felt like they were speaking a language that he didn't know. He heard the words and repeated them, but he struggled to attach meaning to them. Dream. Road. Mother. He felt that the dream implicated him in some way; there was something he was supposed to do or something he was supposed to know. Maybe it was something that would bring him into the circle of light at the kitchen table. What Bear was saying was more than the sum of its parts, and yet the parts were the only thing that Father Joe could grasp.

Father Joe had come with the intention that he would speak. He had wanted to tell Alice that he had interpreted Bear's map and figured out where Bear was, that he gone to Gayle's, that he had struggled with whether to tell Alice about it because it had been a secret and he'd wanted to protect the boy's timing and his privacy, but that had suddenly seemed all wrong. He had wanted to confess all of this. He'd driven over in a snowstorm so as not to waste a single second, and he'd practiced his speech the whole way. But now, just as quickly, his speech was irrelevant. The conversation had moved past him, away from him, beyond him. He could see that this had nothing to do with his confession.

"I saw her twice," Bear said. "Both times she was walking. Both times she was on a road. Both times she was alone. But one time, it seemed like there was someone else nearby. Maybe." Bear paused again and turned his face toward the carpet near where Father Joe sat. "Maybe it was you." Father Joe understood that he was the person meant. In the dream of Bear's mother, he had been nearby. Maybe. Punctuated with the word "maybe."

Father Joe felt the room like a pinball machine, trajectories, vectors, things bouncing off one another to hit other things. Directions attempted and then thwarted. A single silver ball searching for a hole. He saw himself as one of those flippers that flicked at an instant to keep the game alive a little longer, to save the game's demise.

"There's one more thing," Alice said.

She nodded at Bear, who again found his voice.

"Vincent told me about the night Albert died. He said that they were jumped coming out of a bar in Rapid City. He said a bunch of white honkeys came out of nowhere with their knives and stuff. He said the fight was real bad. He said that when the police came, they didn't stop it. They jumped in and started beating the Indian guys too. And one of them, he kicked Albert in the head, a bunch of times."

Bear pulled his legs up on the chair and put his head down on them. Father Joe found himself trying to imagine this boy stabbing Vincent with the man's own knife. What did it feel like to put a knife into another person's flesh, to feel the flesh give way, and then to stab again? How did you know when to stop? There was such a fine line between causing death and causing pain, one small shift of the knife. It was impossible for him to imagine the boy doing this, and yet his mind went there again and again as he looked at the boy's hands and imagined them bloodied.

"Vincent told me," Bear said to his knees. "That day by the creek."

"And you didn't tell anyone?" Bear shook his head, his hair loose around his face. Father Joe felt an urge to take the boy for a haircut, then wondered at this irrelevancy—how it emerged out of nowhere and yet stayed with him as a powerful desire.

Father Joe turned to Alice. Again he felt the pinball moving among the obstacles, lighting them up, moving erratically, still searching, searching for a place to fall.

"What are we supposed to do with this information?" He felt like Alice was hiding something from him. She knew something he needed to know. What she knew was vital, full of power, and if she would tell him, then he could perform the role that was being asked of him. Instead she left him sitting there, bewildered, flicking in blindness.

When his question was met with their mutual silence, when he had waited as long as he could stand, he stood up and pulled his gloves out of his pockets. He pulled the hood of his coat up against the storm. They sat staring at him in perfect stillness, as if waiting for him to answer his own question or as if his leaving was somehow its answer.

"Let's talk tomorrow, then," he said, and went out into the snow-swirled darkness.

Dear Veronica,

I think what I wanted to say, what I am trying to say, is that the vocation of a priest is a conflicted one. Maybe you know this, having watched priests all of your life. But I want to tell you how I see it. I hear confessions. That means that I am accustomed to knowing the lives of others, even in intimate details, knowing even the worst of them without ever speaking about it. It's a sacred calling. It's a way of life. But it also becomes a habit of the strangest sort. I hold myself apart so that I can maintain in silence all that is handed to me. In the early days of the priesthood, I would sometimes think, "If you only knew what I knew." But then after a while, even those kinds of thoughts faded, and I lived as though I had no special information about anyone. In the movies, confessions are treated as deep dark secrets, but most of

the time it's petty stuff. It's easy to forget. Most of the time people
have ways of talking around their confessions and then calling
it done anyway. In truth, all of us are pretty mute about sin. But
my response is the same in any case: silence.

To betray these confidences would be a betrayal of my calling.
Everyone agrees about that, right? Silence is my calling; speaking
is a betrayal. But what if silence is the betrayal and speaking
is the calling? How would someone, trained in silence as I have
been, know when and how to speak?

Fearing you will betray one confidence, you keep them all. And
you can't remember if someone told you something within the
confines of the confessional or if you learned of it by other means.
So you learn to hold everything in some secret container in your
psyche. The more you pile in there, the less human you become.
This is why you don't want to draw close to me, Veronica. I warn
you. The man has been diminished, even as his office has grown
strong. The man longs to be restored, but he does not know whom
to ask or how to speak.

A woman on the road. Father Joe somewhere nearby. Both Bear
and Alice seemed to take these ephemeral glimpses as some
kind of fact. They were asking him for something in relation to
these images, and it was maddening to have no idea what it was.

The next day, he still avoided the packet of letters and turned
to his translation. This time, though, he decided to ask. This
time the translation would be a kind of prayer. Not an escape,
not a place to hide from what was being asked of him, but a way
to address it directly. The psalms were the only way he knew to
address ineffability. They were what he knew of that wordless
place, away from him, where Alice and Bear were.

The letters from Father Fabian and the guest books were in
the box next to his desk, and they had a kind of fetid energy that
demanded his attention. But reading them would change every-

thing. There would be a before-reading and an after-reading—
he knew this intuitively. And if he could just avoid that moment
of change.

He had arrived in his systematic way at Psalm 52, and it did
not look promising for this new intention. In fact it sounded like
a voice of accusation. To make matters worse, the title of the
psalm in his trusty Jerusalem Bible was "The Fate of Cynics."
Wasn't that what Alice had often accused him of? A form of cynicism? And wasn't that what was stopping him now as he faced
the testimony of Bear's dreams? It felt a bit mocking of the Al-
mighty to have inspired him to use the psalms for prayer only to
have the psalm feel like accusation.

"Why make a boast of your wickedness, you champion of vil-
lainy, all day plotting destruction?" He wondered if he should
skip it. He was looking for inspiration here, for understanding,
for help, for God's sake. How was it going to help to be plunged
into accusation? He paged ahead. Psalm 53: "The fool says in
his heart, 'There is no God.'" Great. Psalm 54 looked a little
more promising, "God, save me by your name." But he felt, on
the edges of his consciousness, a tiny voice whispering. He decided to go back and confront "the fate of cynics," wherever that
took him.

He started with the superscription. The psalm was a "Maskil
of David." *Maskil* was a mysterious word. Father Joe wrote it at
the top of his legal pad. No one was quite sure what it meant.
Some said it meant "wise"—a psalm meant to instruct. Others
said it meant "meditation"—inviting contemplation. Some said
it meant "song," with no special meaning. Then the notes offered
a moment in the story of David to consider. "When Doeg the
Edomite went and warned Saul, 'David has gone to Ahimelech's
house.'"

David was on the run from Saul, the king, who was after him.
Saul wanted to kill him; he'd gotten obsessed with the fragil-

ity of his own power and blamed David. David knew he was in danger and was on the run, but he hadn't yet decided if he was going to challenge the king directly, with his own army. In public David was still a friend of the king. So while he hid, David, the singer and writer of songs, paused to put words to what was on his mind while he hid in the house of Ahimelech. Little did he know that Doeg the Edomite was already informing on him. Saul was headed his way.

They didn't sing this kind of thing in church nowadays. It didn't lend itself to four verses and four-part harmony. Not that St. Rose had had a director of music ever—or at least as long as Father Joe had known the place—but you couldn't imagine that person tuning up the piano to sing, "Why do you boast of evil?" Nowadays songwriters tended to focus on victories already won, on good feelings, on comfort and safety and certainty. Here was a different kind of song that came from the heat of things, from the time of unknowing.

The psalms didn't sing like Christians sang. They sang from the sweaty, bloody midst. It reminded Father Joe a little bit of the heated, heavy days of Wounded Knee, those months when AIM had gone to Washington, DC, the "Trail of Broken Treaties," as they'd called it. They'd sat out on the lawn in front of the Bureau of Indian Affairs with their drums. They sang from the midst.

If they had gathered to sing Psalm 52, they would have known exactly who they were singing about. "You who boast of evil. You who devise works of deceit. You who love falsehood. You who abandon the poor. You who love riches more than God." All of these things could definitely be sung with drums and an offbeat in the style of the Lakota.

It's true that those tense and difficult days when violence begat violence had led to some changes. But life on the reservation was as hard as it had ever been. This nation within a nation, where the best of everything has already been given away. The sunsets are free. The wind. But everything else has already been siphoned off: the water, the animals, the jobs.

The most important question anyone could think to ask about Bear was: Was this boy Sioux? If he was, then the tribal courts could "decide" his fate. If he wasn't, then the federal courts had the right to decide. But the state and the feds didn't want anything to do with this kid. They wanted things lined up properly so as to keep power well concentrated. They didn't care about a kid who'd stabbed an Indian guy. This was an Indian guy who'd seen the police kill his friend. They probably wanted him dead anyway. And even more important, they didn't want Windy Creek to have jurisdiction over the ranches in Windy Creek County, on land leased from the tribes or the path by which oil flowed through the reservation. Bear's best chance, Father Joe knew all the way down to the toes in his socks, was with the tribe, if only because it would keep him close to home.

Father Joe would have to ask Alice if there were any "O you who are evildoers" songs in Lakota. On the other hand, Alice might think it bad luck to use one's voice like that. To conjure up evil by speaking its name. Many of the songs call animals or spirits close, and who wants a spirit of evil close at hand? "A word has a soul." Where had he read that recently? It always felt like that with the Hebrew, the way the words rose up from the page with their stolid little bodies, ensouled presences, ready to speak.

So what did this psalm mean, if it was his prayer? What did it mean for the woman on the road, alone, vulnerable, with the snow swirling around her, maybe seeking shelter? Bear's mother, maybe. At the end of the psalm, there was the image of an olive tree, planted, rooted—it is implied that the speaker of the psalm, that thin and lonely "I" of the psalm, is the tree. Even though David was on the run, he imagined himself as a rooted tree, planted in trust, planted in love. Though rootless, rooted. Though cast out, welcomed in. Though rejected, loved.

Father Joe didn't know where to locate himself in the psalm. Was he among the evildoers? Was he singing with the warriors? Was he the planted tree? In David's small gathering ragtag army or in Saul's? "Whose side are you on, Joe?" This is how prayer was. Always, always more questions than answers.

And where was the woman? Who was the woman? What did it mean that he was near her?

17

Known and Unknown

THE NEXT DAY the snow continued. Father Joe adjusted the transistor in the kitchen in the morning to hear the weather forecast, moving the antenna around for a signal. He finally caught it: several feet of snow expected in western South Dakota, the man said through the crackle. Snow continuing through-out the day and into the night. Father Joe tromped down to the church early, with snow above his ankles, to open it for mass, and no one came. The roads were blocked. No plows had been out. Lydia called the church to say that she couldn't get out, but that she hoped Father Joe could survive on the cold meatloaf she'd left. "Heat it up in a pan," she said. "For five minutes with a little water." He thanked her.

In his office, Father Joe had the feeling that there was nowhere to run. There was no maintenance needed on a building that would be closing; no one was going to turn up asking for his advice; anything he said to himself now about things he had to do besides read these letters was a lie. The thought was slightly suffocating, like the snow outside, sealing him in. But there was nothing else to do, so he turned to the letters. He took the top one from the stack and smoothed out its rolled edges. When that was unsuccessful, he hooked the thin paper under the

Jerusalem Bible and held it down so that he could do his best with the fuzzy blue ink.

"Remember, Joe," he said out loud, hearing his voice echo back in the muffled air. "This is about finding the woman on the road. It's not about you."

In the first letter from the stack, Fabian was writing about needing a coach and a librarian at the school. It felt too hot in the office. Father Joe unhooked his collar that he had put on in the morning out of habit and laid it next to the letter on the desk. He rubbed his neck where the collar had been.

Father Fabian had typed:

Speaking of librarians, is there any chance of Father Crowley being assigned to us as a librarian? I don't know the whole story about his departure from St. James. I heard something about a seminary retreat that went awry? Some people in the bushes on the grounds? But I did meet him at Creighton U. He expressed a real desire to come to Blessed Sacrament, and I would love to see him again. We could use him, and I feel sure that we can get along well with him.

Father Dayton has slipped rapidly in recent months. We think he might have had a slight stroke in late May, but the doctor in Hanson did not confirm it. He is very forgetful and also very critical of all the work here. I wonder, if it isn't too presumptuous, if there might not be a priest's home for him somewhere.

———

Father Dayton. Joe remembered him well. A grumpy, slumped man before the stroke and then bitter and impossible after. Father Joe had seen his obituary in the diocesan newsletter a year or two ago. Where had they sent him? The one thing Joe had liked about him was that he hadn't been in Fabian's fan club. It was always nice to have that kind of camaraderie, however silent. But no wonder Fabian wanted to be rid of him. Fabian was doling out gossip on everybody. Father Joe skimmed for his own name. He half expected to appear, even though he was not a Jesuit, a simple parish priest, peripheral to all the goings-on at the school. Fabian only mentioned people if he wanted to elevate or knock down. If they served his purposes.

Bill Laderman was really high in late June. He was trying to get along on four or five hours of sleep a night, staying up to watch all of those late night TV shows. He said he was watching them because he said he would "relate better to the world." And then we found him out roaming around after hours with a boy from the school. I think he might be a bit out of control. I've told him he needs to grow up and be a man about this.

———————

Joe could hear the chuckle and felt a little churn in his stomach. He wasn't sure if it was his own dislike of Fabian or the images of Bear that came into his mind as he read about the "boy" that Bill Laderman was "out with." The tall trees on the grounds of the school. The outbuildings. The shadows and behind them the open, endless night sky of the prairie. The letter went on like this, with the intimate politics of the school, and Fabian's spinning web of self-righteousness.

Focus on the girls, Joe told himself. These letters were before Flynn's arrival, so Father Joe skimmed 1969 for the name of or reference to any girl. He couldn't help being struck that there was no mention at all. No runaways. No top achievers. No girls in trouble. No teachers, barely even nuns. Nothing. Only men. Gary Brown and Bill Laderman, John O'Malley, the math teacher, the maintenance man, Brother Fred—all men with whom Fabian contended, praised, liked, hated, recommended leave, recommended stay. The girl-child Alice was looking for, the woman on the road, she would never make it into Fabian's consciousness or onto these pages. She would have been nothing more than a piece of lint on Fabian's silk socks.

After skimming 1969, he started in on 1970. Flynn, he remembered, arrived in July of that year. Not that it mattered now. That's what he was looking for in 1973. Now—stay focused—she is the one who matters.

In March, Fabian finally mentioned girls. He was writing about Brother Gerald, whom the priests called Brother Jerry. Brother Jerry had a pockmarked face and deep rivets in his bulbous nose from a lifetime of drinking, like his liver had gotten sick of such ill treatment and come to sit on his face. At the same time, he was a relatively cheerful man, even jovial. Joe couldn't say he was well liked, but he was well tolerated. People tended to look the other way when his breath smelled of alcohol at 9 a.m.

Brother Gerald has had his problems—drinking to excess, fooling around with little girls. He had them down in the basement of our building after dark. We've been finding panties here and there, including in the basement. Up to his tricks. And he's been giving out food and smokes at the back door after hours and then disappearing. Before he left on his retreat, I had a nice talk with him on these points, and he took it all decently. I let him know that his position here is certainly threatened, were these things to become known. What I am concerned about is that he is not well, mentally. I think he needs help.

A vein in Joe's forehead started to pound. He saw how tight his fingers had become on the paper. He looked down at his own knuckles, white, the fingers red with the strain. He let go, and the paper rolled up again in the position it had held for ten years. The feeling he had was as if watching a kaleidoscope spin, all the colors becoming hazy while the old pattern breaks apart, but before a new one emerges. He'd wanted these letters as a record of Fabian's abuse of power, as a record of his poor maintenance of the school. He'd wanted them to show Fabian's superiors that it wasn't all sunshine and roses at Blessed Sacrament. He'd wanted evidence to get rid of Flynn because he had kept that man's secrets for too long and they had eroded him. Joe hadn't wanted him to do his damage on Windy Creek.

But now he saw something else: they knew. They hadn't sent Flynn to the reservation by accident. They'd sent him on purpose. And it wasn't just Flynn, and it wasn't just Fabian. They were all playing their games with children in the dark. And everybody knew the whole time—except, somehow, him.

Fabian thought so little of it that he wrote about it in his letters to his superiors. They felt so safe in their little world that they weren't keeping secrets. Not from each other anyway. What they were doing was protecting Flynn. Helping him.

Had Joe known and also not known at the same time? This pretending and shuffling men around as they got into trouble, sending them off to the reservation when things got too hot in that other world—the one they thought was real—and then ignoring and ignoring and ignoring. The sickness ran like the stink of rot through everything, and yet somehow he'd not smelled it, like a background color running through a landscape and yet unseen, like a sound that once heard could not be unheard. The thought that he might be an innocent they could manipulate was as abhorrent to him as the thought that he had looked the other way.

He stood. He walked over to the window and watched the iced-over creek silently disappearing under the snow. He opened the door to his office and walked into the hall. Then he turned and walked back into his office. He took his coat, but didn't put it on, and walked out into the snow, feeling the flakes on his hot face. He left the door of the church wide open, as if he wanted the blizzard to enter it, and trudged, soaking his pants above the knee, up the path toward the rectory. His house. Not his house. Their house. His legs felt strange, like maybe standing was not a good idea. His wing tips and slacks grew wetter and wetter as he took the path, which wasn't even a path now.

Words flitted in and through his consciousness. These weren't ordinary words. They were charged, lit. *Panties. Basement. Nice talk.* He pictured that basement of the school as it was now—windows smashed out, trash scattered across its floor, abandoned, hulking, and haunted. Everyone had moved on to the new school, but no one had moved on at all. No wonder. No wonder. But he didn't have other words. He couldn't replace them with anything that could explain it.

Joe couldn't say any of the sentences or even phrases to himself in full. He couldn't repeat *fooling around with little girls.* He couldn't say *had them in the basement.* But as the snow soaked his pant legs and numbed his feet, he repeated *become known.* So that was it, then. That was the issue. Back then, he had thought that the becoming known was the part he was going to play. He thought he was going to use it to take down Fabian, get Flynn sent away. *Sent away where, Joe? Where did you think they were going to put him?*

When the school leadership changed, he'd thought there was no need for it to become known because Fabian and company had all left, and what would be the point? But *they*—the hierarchy, the monsignors, the bishops, and the archbishops—were the ones he'd thought needed to know. He had imagined that once they knew, they would do something about it. They would say, "Well, obviously, this can't go on." But what they'd said in essence was "Don't let it become known." That was even, he could see it now, the message that they'd sent him. Here's a nice place on Windy Creek for you, Father Joseph. You seem like the hermit type. It's nice and quiet out there. Don't let anything become known.

And yet how strange it was: Fabian had actually written Brother

Gerald's crimes, Laderman's crimes, and who knows what else, down in black and white. And he'd invited more. What did *send Father Crowley* mean, if it didn't mean more conspirators, more people who understand us. No inner black pit of the confessional, as Joe had tried to explain to Veronica. Joe had carried around Flynn's secret like some festering coal, lost his job for it, lost his career—at least as his mother had imagined it—and they hadn't sacrificed Flynn. They'd elevated him and sacrificed Joe instead. Because they'd always known. Flynn was on Windy Creek not because they had needed to know and Joe had needed to tell them, but because they knew, and they wanted to put him somewhere were things *wouldn't become known.* Bad publicity, that's what all of this came down to.

Joe could see his own ambition now. He laughed darkly. Be a good priest. Be a good man. Fulfill his calling. He'd accepted their praise: "Tough assignment you've got there, Kreitzer." How many back-slapping conversations had he had with Fabian? How many times had he teased Fabian about how he dressed like the pope was going to show up for study hall? How had they lived, exactly, in this kind of darkness and blindness? He felt like the word "mission" might explain it all.

He could see how they played him. God, they were good, weren't they. They knew you. They knew how to buy your silence and have you say it was worth the price. It wasn't outrage that Joe felt; it was shame.

He hadn't found Bear's mother. But he had found her story.

He wretched, a sudden and shocking rising of bile, but his vomit was quickly covered over by the falling snow.

18

These Little Ones

THE RECTORY WAS dark and cold. When Father Joe arrived, the light of the short day was dimming. He took off his shoes and socks and walked barefoot across the kitchen, mindless of the numbness in his toes. He felt a strong desire to get on the road, to go somewhere, go anywhere, beyond the limits of the bishop, all the bishops, wherever that was, where the church had no sway, couldn't decide for him, how things would be. Hadn't that once been part of the charm of his life? That the church was everywhere in everything, and he was connected to it? Now he didn't want any kind of connection at all. He wondered where he could go, where they weren't. He'd tried to write to Veronica: the ocean. Could he get there?

He looked out the window at the spindly trees in an ever-growing expanse of white. He pictured himself at the Chute in Hanson, without his collar on, ordering a beer. He would be recognized immediately. He pictured himself driving out into the storm without a thought about where it would take him or where he would go, driving and driving, with snow drifts making irregular obstacles in the road, the night around him dense and unending. He pictured himself at that cabin Veronica had mentioned near Spearfish.

He poured himself a glass of whiskey and sat down on the couch in the formal living room, his wet pants clinging to his naked calves. He should change his pants. Put on warm socks. He sat very still for a moment, the cold in his feet overtaking his whole body in a blessed numbness. The room darkened into shadows. The whiskey burned all the way down in his body's one sign of life.

He stayed in that spot for several hours. Eventually, he started thinking and thinking, as if thinking were a survival response instead of a torture device. Our trouble came, he thought, from ourselves—from our love for hierarchy, from our desire to follow a known way. It came right from those great Gothic cathedrals and their orders of angels. How we wanted to be right and to be good and to be well ordered. How right we thought we were. But when it came time to speak, we didn't have words. When it came time to challenge, we had only atrophied muscles in our throats. We thought we were good soldiers in a holy war, and it turned out that we were rank and file with no mind of our own. Bees in a hive. Ants on a hill. But we weren't wholly insects because we had put our mental skills to plenty of use in the work of self-protection.

We were taught the skills of self-analysis: how to search our souls, he thought. From way back we'd learned to number our sins, one at a time. In the old, old days, when the rite of confession had first been invented, monks had confessed several times a day so that hours wouldn't pass without absolution. Was that how it evolved, from the very acts of confession, from grace itself? The ones trapped inside dark desires could confess them again and again inside the enclosure that the priesthood created and be absolved again and again, inside that same enclosure. And because it was the only enclosure that mattered, because everyone else was on a path of sin obviously far greater than ours and came to us again and again for forgiveness, we dispensed forgiveness by habit, by rote. *In the stead and by the command of my Lord Jesus Christ I forgive you all your sins in the name of the Father and the Son and the Holy Ghost. Amen.*

What was supposed to be freedom became a trap. What was supposed to be love became a coldness of heart that became so frozen, it could endure any heat and remain itself, trapped in the darkness.

How else could you explain us, Father Joe thought. How could you make sense of our great silence, our tremendous, world-shattering silence that tried to uphold what could not hold? *But whoso shall offend one of these little ones which believe in me, it were better for him that a millstone were hanged about his neck, and that he were drowned in the depth of the sea.*

For so long we pointed at them, he thought. We said: Look at how they are overtaken by violence. Look at how they need our help for even the most basic things. Look at how they drink to excess and how they treat their women. Look at the poverty in them. His colleagues, their books and papers and histories full of advice on how to catechize the Lakota. "It's like pissing into the wind," one of his colleagues had said to him privately. The old men in black celebrated Father Joe because he stayed, because he endured what in their minds couldn't be endured. A man needed to feel some progress in his work, needed to feel he was going somewhere, doing something. Father Joe had some-how managed to live without that feeling, and so they called it "Christlike" when they wrote it up in their press releases. But that was only another way to avoid looking to themselves.

We relied on our paperwork. We relied on our procedures and on our authority and on our rituals of self-forgiveness, he thought. Everything, everything but what mattered.

The people didn't need us to tell them that they were frag-ile. That they needed forgiveness. That essential message of the Christian faith—that you are sinners and you need to repent—of what use was that to the people of Windy Creek as they watched their world be evacuated from under their feet, each interaction a loss?

But a few you could convince, and then there were certain

rituals that the devout came to rely on, to give them solace in a world being torn away. And so the priests filled an office, a function. A priest didn't speak with his own voice, words that were his and expressed his own feelings and thoughts. That was not how this worked. You spoke the words of the office, of the church. You were official—as in of the office. The closer you could come to speaking in and through the office, the better you were doing your job.

No one talked about the effect of this on your voice, your own voice's erosion. How good you become at saying the things everyone expects you to say. How smooth. How light. In this, Father Joe and Fabian were not so far apart.

And you know what? Father Joe's mind was heating now, spinning, spooling out thought as though it might protect him, the way a caterpillar sends out threads for its cocoon. Vatican II made all of this worse. You would think it would have made things better. Father Joe had been in favor. He'd read every word that issued from the councils, made the changes right away, convinced they would help him reach the people. Reach the people. Mission, again. The bile in his throat rose. But it actually intensified the problem, because with services in the vernacular, now your vernacular speech got sucked up into the machine even as the machine became more machine like. Before, when the masses were in Latin, maybe you could have two voices: a church voice and an outside-of-church voice, and you could hold them apart from one another, but now there was only one voice.

But for decades, all his life really, the choices of someone like Flynn or Brother Gerald had seemed like someone else's problem and someone else's realm. Not that he didn't know about them. He knew there were priests that didn't live up to their callings; of course he did. But ultimately he saw now, he believed, the hierarchy would take care of it. His realm was to be as good a priest as he could be. His realm was to follow the call of Jesus as he saw it in the best people around him. Light bulbs and homilies. Roof repair and psalms. But then it all came back to silence: silence was what he did for a living. He was trained to speak in only very circumscribed ways, hemmed in by the demands of the office. He'd kept the secrets of others by profession. And so. *Little girls. Panties. Basement.*

Eventually he fell asleep on the couch with the whiskey bottle next to him. He drifted in and out of sleep, craving a blanket one minute and disappearing into sleep the next. He dreamed that he was playing poker in a darkened room, like a Rembrandt painting, all shadows and half-lit faces, the light from some unknown source falling on the poker chips. He could almost smell the cigar smoke, the whiskey. Fabian was there, with other men, around the table, all of them dressed in black, wearing collars.

He was losing to Fabian. Again and again. Fabian swept the chips toward him with his fine hand, glittery with rings. The cards were shuffled and dealt, faster and faster. Losing and losing. His chest felt tight. He couldn't breathe. He woke up gasping, his tongue thick with whiskey.

For the next several hours, Joe's mind was filled with acts of violence. Ways that he might kill Fabian, for somehow he was convinced that Fabian was to blame for all of it. He represented them all down to the last one. He pictured old-style duels on a Deadwood street, the two of them with pistols. He pictured punching him. He tried out other more abstract forms of murder: poisoning, sneaking around the back of his house with a gasoline can. But it was the personal images of violence that captured his imagination, a desire to leave the man bloodied. Even so, the images had elements of farce in them.

He fell asleep again toward morning, and this time his dream was stranger and more abstract. He was on a cliff above the sea in the midst of a terrible storm. Waves were thundering against the cliff. Looking out into the sea, Joe could see cars that had been flooded and were being tossed by the waves. The cars would emerge from the waves and then submerge again. There must be many dead. He wondered why he had not heard reports.

Then he saw a body float from one of the cars, toward the shore. He climbed down the steep slope and pulled the body from the water onto a beach of small gray stones. It was the body of a man, more dead than alive. In the dream, Joe somehow carried the man up the steep slope and took him to an apartment in a city. They were on a high floor looking out over vast twinkling lights. The apartment seemed to be all windows.

Joe laid the man on the floor and began to remove his wet clothing. First, his shoes and socks. Then his shirt and pants, his boxers, until he was a naked, pale heap. All the time, he was asking himself, "Is this how it is done? Am I doing this right?" Then he dragged the man into the bathroom and put him in a tub of warm water. He felt intense, overwhelming love for this man, and he found that he didn't care if the man lived or died. He only wanted to love him. Another part of his mind spoke continually, "You do not know who he is."

The man woke. He looked around. "This is a nice apartment," he said. It was Fabian.

––––––

Joe woke sore and crusty. Light was coming in from the front windows. He roused himself from the couch and went to look out at the world, gleaming with bright sunshine. It was stark and silent, a perfect, untouched blanket of snow under a blue sky. He had slept through mass. The sunlight made that obvious. But no one had knocked on the door and that made him think that no one had ventured out.

He roused himself and showered to try to take the sour smell off. Before he left for the church, he got out an extension cord from a bottom drawer in the kitchen and plugged the Buick into an outlet on the house. It was possible the car wouldn't even start. His gestures had become methodical, as if he had decided something he didn't even know he had decided.

Then he put on his boots and walked down to the church. The first thing he noticed was one set of footprints in the snow. They led up to the steps and then back, pushing the snow back a bit into a kind of path leading to and from a set of tire tracks. Someone had, in fact, come for mass and found the door open and Father Joe nowhere to be found. He felt a flip-flop of shame in his stomach. It must have been Alice.

When he walked into the church, he saw Alice's altar cloth on the altar. It lay gleaming and almost alive with its swirls of color. Each bead and quill caught light from the window and sparkled. She had laid it over the old altar cloth so that it was rimmed with a rich purple and then she had set the good silver chalice and paten on top, as if waiting for some other Father Joe to arrive. Maybe it was an older version of himself, one that knew how to arrange the divine mysteries. Or it was some future version, healed and whole. It certainly wasn't this one, shaggy and lost, having fought all night with ghosts and come out limping.

Father Joe went up to the altar and stood in front of it, admiring what she had done. Even while he had been doing nothing but grieving, feeling sorry for himself, and drinking, she'd been turning straw into gold. As he stared at the altar, he saw a feather lying next to the chalice. It was not large, flecked with gold and orange and brown, with a pattern of black lines running through it that reminded Joe of both text and wings within wings. Thinking of walks with Bear as a child, he recognized it as a feather from a red-tailed hawk.

He reached for the feather and put it in the pocket of his shirt. Then, feeling the texture and presence of the silent air, he turned and walked out.

PART III

Heart Dance

SIOUX FALLS, SOUTH DAKOTA

1983–1984

19

Vast

OUT ONTO HIGHWAY 44, Joe turned east. Sioux Falls was almost four hours directly east of Windy Creek. First there were
the wide sand hills with their new snow crust that drifted
onto the highway, the bluffs dropping sharply toward the great
river, then miles and miles of squared-off land, fence posts poking through snow drifts, a farmhouse here and there. This is
how you knew you'd hit one hundred percent white people's
land: the careful demarcations. Joe thought of his grandparents
and the way that they had staked claim onto a great wide nothing. They'd said, in effect, to their other neighbors, with a lot of
help from the government: this patch of nothing will be mine
and that patch of nothing will be yours. And so it was.

In Joe's family there was a story about how the family had
come to the Dakotas. His grandfather had come from Germany,
broken and poor, having spent every penny on the trip, and
when he arrived in New York, the officials there had handed
him a train ticket and said "This way" in a way that made him
to understand that he should follow. He hadn't even spent
one full night in America when he'd found himself on a train
headed west with people who spoke no common language. The
train barreled across the continent, deeper and deeper into the

unknown, while his grandfather watched out the window at the strange land. The sun went down and came up and went down and came up while he marked the days by scratching marks on the train seat. He'd had two sandwiches and a tin of sardines, which were long gone by the third day. Where could they be going? He'd never known a land so large. He kept thinking, "How vast, how vast."

Then in the middle of one night—when he'd thought they never would reach their destination, when he'd begun to think there really wasn't a destination and he had somehow found himself in the middle of a dream from which he could not wake up—he was jolted awake by the train stopping. "Everybody out! Everybody out!" the conductor had called, and the man had no words in English to protest or ask for an explanation. In other languages, he heard passengers stir and ask each other what must have been questions like "Where are we? Does anyone know? What will become of us?" They were unloaded onto a platform that was a few planks nailed together in the midst of tall grass. On a makeshift pole, a sign read MUSKEYVILLE. The man huddled in the grass next to the "station" with his fellow shipwrecked passengers while the train continued on into the night. Above them was a sky more full of stars than they had ever imagined, around them wave after wave of grass.

The train had dropped them off in the middle of Dakota Territory. Someone's harebrained plan to build the frontier and save the cities from immigrants and foreigners by shipping new arrivals west while also claiming territory for Europeans. Make a living. Make a life. Trains going back the other direction were rare. And so, they'd begun.

Joe didn't really have much of a plan for himself as he drove east into a now bright sun. He was acting mechanically, fulfilling his longing from the night before to drive away. But his plans did not include a driving to. While he drove, he took off his collar and unbuttoned his black shirt. Everything about him still said "priest," he thought. He should have worn different clothes. It hadn't occurred to him until now that there must be laypeople's clothes at the back of his closet somewhere. Maybe he could buy some at a thrift store in Sioux Falls. Would it make a difference or was there a priestliness already on him like a vapor? Maybe there was no changing out of it. No pretending to be someone else.

But if you couldn't change the man, maybe you could change the place. Sioux Falls was more absence than presence, more appealing for what it wasn't than for what it was. It was not the diocese of Rapid City. It was not Windy Creek. It was a place where the question "Whose side are you on?" had less sway, less immediate power. But there was also the fact that Veronica was close by. She had said St. Mary's Sioux Falls was her parish. Harrisburg was a little hamlet outside Sioux Falls, bordered by cornfields on all sides. Maybe he could go and park outside her house, not even go in. Park and wait and think in the clear, frigid air.

What was his aim? he wondered. It was strange to be out in the world without one. He touched the hawk feather in his pocket and tried to remember what Alice had told him and Bear back in their days of feather hunting about the meaning of the hawk feather. He knew it was sacred, a feather used at ceremonies, but as usual, he couldn't remember the details. Each bird feather had a different meaning. A hummingbird feather—extremely rare—signified time outside time. A raven feather was a kind of warning. But what was the hawk? And was a red-tailed hawk distinct from other hawks? Was it something about protection? Courage? Communication? It was frustrating to now have this talisman and not know what it meant. Maybe if he had paid better attention, he would now have some direction, some instruction.

Then it occurred to Joe that maybe the feather hadn't been intended for him. He'd scooped it up and put it in his pocket with such certainty that Alice was communicating with him when, in fact, he had no evidence that this was the case. That flip-flop of shame came again. What if she had left that feather on the altar as a prayer, as supplication, as an offering, and he had assumed it belonged to him? Shoved it in his pocket like he was trying to keep it a secret. He should have left it there. He should drive back right now and replace it. Shame. Shame. He kept driving.

He slowed down through the occasional small town, noting the grain elevator, the diner, the water tower with the town's name neatly stenciled on it. In Parkston, he pulled into a gas station for a pit stop and a cup of bad coffee. This, he thought as he sipped the dark liquid in Styrofoam, is not what Gayle called the fuel of the full blood—pejuta sapa—black medicine. This was closer to what he called cat piss. The young woman behind the counter at the gas station had painted each fingernail on her hand a different color, he noticed. The paint was chipped and the nails a little chewed. But the effect did make Joe wonder about her while she rang him up with put-on disinterest.

As he drove on, turning slightly north and then east again on Highway 42, he thought about how the structure of his life had been built to allow certain things in and to block other things out—an architecture. Once you've lived in the house for a while, you forget about all the things it doesn't allow you to see. You forget that any house, every house, has blind spots, and what you know is always partial. Pretty soon you see only what you are used to seeing and hear only what you are used to hearing. If other things are happening around you but they don't fit what you've planned to see and hear, they might as well not exist to you. Maybe this is what the old saying "He who has ears let him hear" means. You are being asked to see beyond what you already know. Not everybody has the ears to hear or the eyes to see.

An hour outside Sioux Falls, Joe at last turned on the radio. He'd been willing himself to allow the silence, almost as a kind of penance for the night of distracted desperation. But now he flipped through stations, tuning the radio dial with his right hand. He heard Jefferson Airplane. On another station, Chuck Berry. On another station, he paused while an old-time gospel-hour preacher exhorted the radio audience in a voice that almost sounded like a chant. If you didn't listen to the words and caught the cadences as they rose and fell, it sounded like a kind of music. It was a recitation almost as rhythmic as a Gregorian chant. But the incantation riled Joe up rather than calmed him. If there had been a station playing chant, that might have been a nice intervention. Stealing into the heart, expanding it a little. This was more like an agitation, an incitement.

He crossed over the Big Sioux, now mostly ice. Civilization suggested itself in slightly denser houses, almost, but not quite yet, like neighborhoods. Over the bridge he pulled over to take a moment to breathe and to think.

That's when he saw her: a child in his rearview mirror. She was walking along the side of the highway in black pants and a long, overly large plaid flannel shirt with no jacket. At first glance, he thought she might be eight or nine years old: too young to be out on the road alone and the weather far too cold, despite the sun, for her to be without a coat. She walked in Moon Boots on the plowed edge of the road, where there was no sidewalk. He looked at the direction from which he had come, trying to imagine from where in that emptiness the girl had emerged. He hadn't seen her when he'd driven by, so she must have reached the road recently. He looked ahead of him at the snowy expanse of highway and tried to imagine where she was going.

She was now approaching at a steady pace. He noticed that every few steps, she would hitch up the straps of her cheap, colorful school backpack, like she feared the straps were slipping or the backpack was heavier than she would like. Each time she made this adjustment, she would then ball up her hands into the long sleeves of the oversize shirt. She was a little overweight in a way that suggested a few too many sweets, with long black hair that she wore in a ponytail at the base of her neck.

When she saw Father Joe in front of her, she looked across the highway as if thinking she might cross to avoid him. He decided to ask her if she needed help. He opened the Buick door.

"Do you need a ride? It's pretty cold," he said, rubbing his hands.

She stopped and eyed him. He could tell she was funneling his question through some mechanism of her own, and that gave him a moment to study her face. It was round and almost moonlike in its placidness. She had glasses and she used the pause in her motion to push them up on her nose, hitch up the backpack straps again, and then bury her hands in the shirt. The patch of skin around one of her eyes was slightly lighter than the rest of her skin, like a patch of bleach. It increased the moon effect of her face. Father Joe, used to life on Windy Creek, found himself studying her for signs of whether she was Indian or not. Her two-tone skin interrupted his usual quick judgments, and he thought how easily he knew his categories: white, full-blood, half-blood. He wondered if those words meant anything to this girl.

She calculated the risk of him, and then made her decision.

"Sure," she shrugged, and walked around to the far side of the Buick. She pulled open the passenger door and loaded her backpack in first and then followed. She sat on her hands, with her backpack between herself and Father Joe.

"Where are we going?" he asked.

"To school."

"Where's that?"

"It's up here a ways. I'll tell you where to turn." Her tone was confident, matter-of-fact.

"Aren't you late?"

"My mom's car wouldn't start this morning. Too cold."

"But your mom didn't walk with you to school?"

"No." The girl looked out the window. "Too cold."

He wanted to say something about a coat and a hat, about the danger of the road, about a girl being on the highway alone, but then he thought better of it.

"I'm Father Joe," he finally said.

"Pleased to meet you," she said in a singsong voice, as if she were reciting something she had heard and practiced.

After that they were silent as they approached the first ragged edge of the city.

"Turn there." She pointed ahead at the first streetlight. "You go left and then right. Are you a priest?"

"Yes."

"I thought that when you said 'Father.' Because you don't look like somebody's father, I mean."

"Oh."

"I mean, you know when fathers look a certain way, and anyways people don't usually say what kind of person they are when they introduce themselves. Like my teacher doesn't say 'Teacher Vandeberg.'" She reasoned all of this out loud, as if Father Joe weren't there and she was thinking into the air. Father Joe felt privileged to be listening in. He was still wondering what she meant by fathers looking a certain way and what kind of fathers she meant. But she was continuing on. "My teacher says to call her "Mrs. Vandeberg. Or sometimes we call her Mrs. V. If she did it your way, she would be Teacher Debra. When she's Mrs. V, then she could be anybody. A nurse or a veterinarian. I want to be a veterinarian. Or the person who takes money at the bank. What do you call that person?"

"A teller."

"A teller. Isn't that a funny word? I mean a teller should be like a person who tells things. It doesn't even mean what it is supposed to mean. Turn here. There's the school." She pointed. Father Joe pulled in along a chain-link fence, where a long, low, blond-brick school stood across a gravel-and-grass playing field.

"Thank you very much," the girl said. The formal tone had re-appeared. She opened the door and grabbed her backpack. Then she paused. "Um . . . can you pick me up again after school?"

"After school?"

"Yeah. I don't know. . . . I don't think my mom's car will be working by then and . . ."

"What time?"

"Three thirty-five," she said.

"Okay," Father Joe said, even though he had no idea where he would be at 3:35.

"Thank you very much." She turned and ran toward the fence's gate and then up the front path toward the school, swinging her backpack from one arm, her feet shuffling on the pavement. He watched her disappear into the school.

20

Butterfly Effect

HE HADN'T EVEN learned her name. He wondered if she had been serious about the pickup. She seemed like a serious child. He felt concerned about her trust of him. A child like her should not be accepting rides from strangers. He thought of children's faces appearing on the back of milk cartons. Kidnapped. And yet, he also felt that this was a child who had her own instincts and trusted them. Another child, he imagined, could have decided not to go to school on such a cold day, with her mother clearly out of commission in some way. But this child had determination. She would go to school and see her Mrs. V., one way or another.

The encounter, and the fact that it was now late morning, made Joe hungry. He decided to get something to eat. He pulled into the parking lot of a diner called the Fryin' Pan and walked stiff-legged and sore to a booth. He ordered the biggest breakfast they had on the menu: bacon and three eggs, three pancakes, buttered toast, and coffee. He ate like it was a ballast against the day. He hadn't eaten like that since, well, since Lydia had taken him off bacon, that's for sure.

He appreciated the anonymity settling over him in the diner. It was almost like a world in which Fabian did not exist. One in which his actions and his choices weren't weighed against the incessant question "Who's side are you on, Joe?"

"I am on that little girl's side," he said to himself. "That's whose side I'm on." The haze of the previous night, the letters, their stink, his conversation with Bear and Alice about Bear's dreams—it all settled away from him, as if it belonged to some other world. In this world, everything was simplified. Eggs, toast, coffee.

How did he want to spend the day before 3:35? Maybe he would go to the new shopping mall and watch passersby. Maybe he would go to a movie, escape into the dark of a theater and even fall asleep. Maybe he could buy a newspaper and sit and read every word of it, in this very diner, until 3:35.

Around him, the day proceeded. Cars sent up slush on Highway 42; two farmers had a conversation about corn prices in the booth behind him. The waitress stood behind the counter, leaning backward on her two hands, her face inscrutable. Crows pecked at a snowbank through the window. Here, unlike on Windy Creek, there was no coherence among all of these things. Each of them was a bit of life. But the waitress had no connection—that he knew of—to the two farmers who had no connection to him who had no connection to the crows. Each random bit was on its own. In such a place, anonymity was possible. It contained a kind of freedom. But he thought, as he ate his pancakes, there was meaninglessness in it too. He all but unconsciously reached up to touch the feather in his pocket. It felt like a talisman from that other world. In that world, each individual action, each encounter, each person had a connection to the broader whole. His work as a priest there was contingent—each action was related to the one before. Albert's death had led to a search for Bear's mother had led to reading the letters had led to . . . And that was the question, what had it led to? It had led him here—to seek a place where no one knew him and no one could judge him. Where contingency could give way for at least a little while.

Meaning was something they made together on Windy Creek. Like Alice attaching one bead to the next with her needle, moving swiftly, seemingly without thought, but with intricacy. He had been woven into the cloth, made a part of things. And now his thread, his strand was ending, about to be cut off. There would be no more Father Joe in the tapestry that was Windy Creek, but the tapestry would go on being made.

But truth—was truth the same as meaning? Was it being made the same way or did it stand apart from their collective efforts, maybe even judging them for the distance they made between meaning and truth? Was truth a cold, hard something that needed to be found like a fact? Or was it a softer something, shaped by them and also shaping them? Or was it a repetition, a tradition? He lifted up the bread of the Eucharist and said, "This is the bread of life," and in that ritual they hit bedrock: truth. Whenever he had said the liturgy at St. Rose, he had always felt like he was speaking continuance and connectedness—over time, over space—and he had long accepted that continuance and connectedness were truth.

But maybe that wasn't it at all. Maybe truth was a lonely road, open and vast, like the one he had been on. Something that you had to walk alone.

Was Alice sitting around, wherever she was right now, wondering about truth? The truth of Bear's mother's identity, the truth of Bear's identity. He doubted it. First of all, she had too many other things to think about: children and grandchildren and Rabbit had lost his job after only a couple of weeks on a construction site, and she didn't know if it had something to do with drinking. Jackie had a new boyfriend, and it was hard to tell if this one was any better. She kept saying that she and the new guy were going to move to Montana. Vincent had been released from the hospital. He would live, but no one had heard from him. His reappearance was a constant worry. Meanwhile, Marlena held it all together with a hint of resentment that she couldn't keep them from falling apart.

Alice had made him feel valuable all of these years. Because she had come to mass and needed what it offered, he had been able to offer it day after day. If doubts arose, because people were going to the Pentecostals, because people were saying that the church didn't belong on the reservation, because he sometimes wanted to see a little more tangible good from his work, he had answered these doubts with Alice's presence.

But the letters raised something that went beyond doubt, beyond things people say. This was more like the smell of something rotten in the refrigerator: the smell tells you that something is truly there. There's no denying it, no debating truth. Laderman up all night watching television. Jerry drinking himself into oblivion, with his crimes unaddressed. Dayton letting his soul pickle with hatred. It wasn't, as he'd always thought, this priest or that priest. The rot went right up the chain.

Amid all of his thoughts, he kept returning to the letters again and again, the way a tongue might return to a broken tooth, compelling the pain forward over and over so he could feel it. Was it still there?

Without him on Windy Creek, the basic functions of the church would go on. People would still be baptized and confirmed, albeit at Blessed Sacrament instead of St. Rose. The mass over at Blessed Sacrament would swell slightly, and Father Driscoll could take credit for the rise in numbers. Nice man. Ten years younger than Father Joe. Supportive of the little Society of St. Vincent de Paul. Consolidation was efficient. The priests were interchangeable. A great assembly line of the soul. Behind it, there was an emptiness, a self-serving emptiness.

Today, more than anything, he wanted to talk about these things with Veronica. If he could. If he could find the words,

fight through all the layers of suffocating silence. Harrisburg—
he consulted the map that he'd brought in from the car—was
only about thirty minutes away from here.

It was near noon when he drove through Sioux Falls. In the
red rock downtown, he spotted a St. Vincent de Paul store, and
he went in and bought a bright pink coat and a hat and gloves.
He saw some light pink snow pants, and he bought those too.
He crossed over the Big Sioux again and turned south toward
Harrisburg. He tried to remember what he had written to Veronica last. How honest had he been? Where in his own search
had he left a marker for her? Now he was dropping in on her, as
she had done with him, without warning. He wondered what he
would say about that. "I just wanted to pick up our conversation"
felt a bit forced, didn't it, especially with what he imagined was
an unusually wild look in his eye.

Harrisburg didn't announce much of a presence. You could
easily miss it. There was a steeple on the horizon and then a
bar kitty-corner from the Food and Fuel. He found the little
snow-rutted country road whose number was familiar to him
from addressing his envelopes to her. There weren't too many
such roads to choose from, and as she'd described, he saw a big
DEKALB sign on one corner and a Lutheran church on the other.
He turned. Past the Lutheran church, there was a grove of bare
hickory trees surrounding a gravel drive, their twisted trunks
sheltering Veronica's house from the wind. Across the road was
the pig farm about which Veronica had written, and he could
hear the clanging of metal in the long, low stable as the pigs
shuffled around in their heated pens. The smell of them was
nostril-constricting even through the rolled-up car windows.

Joe did not turn into the driveway but parked the car along
the hickory trees and thought about what came next. Their letters had taken on a soft, serious, confessional tone, but it wasn't
at all clear how that was supposed to translate to an in-person
conversation. A lot had changed since they'd stood across the

threshold of his door that summer afternoon and said goodbye and let's be friends.

His boots crunched on the snow as he approached the house—a wood-sided ranch house with a porch that stretched the entire length of the front. A wreath hung on the door with fake holly berries and green piping woven through it.

He cleared his throat as he knocked, aware of the coffee acid in his stomach and mouth. Behind the door, he heard movement—footsteps, a rustle. Then the door opened. She looked older than she had that day in the church. Her tangle of curls was piled up on her head. She had glasses perched on her nose, as if she had been reading. She looked at him, startled, and for a few long seconds did not appear to know who he was.

"Joseph," she said finally. She took off her glasses and put them in the pocket of the plain black dress that she was wearing.

"I had to come to Sioux Falls on business," he said. "It was all rather last minute, but I thought I would stop by. I am sorry I didn't call first." He found himself reaching up to touch the hawk feather in his pocket, as if, again, it was offering him some protection in this moment where he suddenly felt naked. It was a half-conscious gesture, but it did help.

"How funny," she said. "I was just about to sit down to write to you." She moved aside from the front of the door in an unspoken invitation.

Her house, he noticed, was not much decorated. There was a vase here, dried flowers there, the smell of eucalyptus from an arrangement near the door. But the furniture looked like it had been in place for decades without much thought given to it. The walls were white and mostly bare. It wasn't exactly neglect, but more of an ambivalence that Joe perceived, an ambivalence about appearances, about the effort that one should put into how things looked.

She led him through the formal living room to the back porch. The Hermitage. He recognized it immediately from her description. There was a stack of books on a small table with a cup of half-drunk coffee on top and another stack of books next to the chair. She had a space heater running, and through the glass, Joe could see a shield of trees, then the meadow and the cornfields under undisturbed snow. On the chair was a pad of stationery and a pen.

"Have a seat," she said, pulling a chair from another corner of the porch. "I'll put on some fresh coffee."

He sat and pulled out the feather from his pocket while she was in the kitchen. She appeared in the doorway above the short, metal-rimmed drop-off to the porch.

"Is it too cold here?" she said. "Would you be more comfortable in the living room?"

"No, no. This is fine."

They both paused, as if nervous.

"Do you know anything about hawks?" he asked suddenly.

"What do you mean?"

"Do you see this? I think it's a redtail." He held out the feather toward her. "I've been wondering what it meant. What it might stand for." He cleared his throat again. The words "stand for" were not quite right. What was he asking her for? Why did he think she might know? The right words were beyond his reach.

She pressed her lips together and reached out her hand for the feather. He gave it to her and felt the space between them decrease to the distance of a few short inches. She pulled her glasses from her pocket and placed the feather in her left palm. It felt odd to him that she was taking his question seriously. He had half expected to be laughed at and dismissed.

In her palm, the feather appeared both dainty and impressive, the ripples of brown and red against a white background, a bit of rust here and there. At the bottom there was a puff of soft white, like a skirt.

"You think," she said at last, "that it's a message?"

"Yes," he said. "Something like that."

She considered this. She lifted her gaze to look out the window, over the glittering expanse.

"What I think of," she said, "is how high a hawk flies. They go up to a great height, to get the lay of the land. I've watched them scope out the fields and the meadows. And then from there, they somehow see exactly what they are looking for. They swoop down fast and grab it."

She handed the feather back. "Did someone give it to you? Did you find it?"

"A little bit of both," Joe said, aware that he was blushing.

She disappeared into the kitchen and returned with a mug of coffee. After she handed it to him, she sat down across from him. He looked out at the glossy snow and tried to think of something to say. The silence had two competing currents. One was a sense Joe had that they'd been talking for thirty years. Everything that had to be said had been said, and they could sit here across from each other like old friends with coffee mugs steaming and watch the snow harden under the glare of the sun. But the other was anxious and edged. Something needed to emerge, and he didn't know how to help it.

"They are sending me to Hastings, Nebraska," he said at last.

"Who?"

"The diocese. The bishop."

"To do what?"

"A church there. Moving a priest out. Moving me in."

She tapped her fingernails on the mug. They made a sharp, clicking sound.

"And St. Rose?" she said.

"Closing." She had a way of making him feel his words more intensely. Until he said it to her, he hadn't felt the pain in it. It had been an abstract reality, full of details and philosophical musings.

"Do you ever get the feeling," she said after a minute, "that we live our lives so that nothing will ever happen? If we had it our way, there would be no plot to the story. Nothing to tell. We'd live so that we'd have no effect on the world. Do you know what I mean? Or maybe you don't live that way, Joseph. Maybe you are the hero of your own story."

She glanced up at him with her gracefully arched eyebrows and smiled. He laughed. It came out as a bit of a snort.

"I've been thinking about all the ways I've tried to avoid life's intrusion. All the barricades I've put up against it. I think I would like to change that. I wonder what it would be like to live a little more rawly, a little closer to the edge."

"Does this have something to do with your book on free will?" He gestured to the piles of books around her.

She laughed. "Classic librarian. Read first. Act later. But I am looking for something, some understanding."

"I don't know," Joe said. "I guess I've been thinking about whether we ever choose anything or if circumstances dictate almost all of it. Aren't we always caught up in forces larger than ourselves? We imagine ourselves acting freely, but sometimes I wonder if that's a presumption of the theologians, something they like to dangle about. You hinted at that in your letter a while back, and I've been thinking about it. They use it to make sure that you know you are a sinner and you have no one to blame but yourself. Meanwhile, the extent of your choices on any given day might boil down to what to eat for breakfast. Cheerios or Shredded Wheat." He laughed. "In my case, Lydia pretty much decides that."

She was listening intently, leaning in. "Are you saying we are puppets, dancing to a tune someone else sets?"

"Maybe not puppets, but actors, with scripts. Reading our lines, performing our roles. Our duties. Our obligations. I mean, if you and I had married, all those years ago, we would have lived a different script than the one we lived. For me, anyway, I would've taken on a different set of duties. I would've sold insurance or something to support you and our children. I'm guessing insurance salesmen also have rituals. They repeat themselves quite a bit, like priests do. Maybe I'm wrong. Someone else would've performed the duties at St. Rose. But how different would the end result have been?"

Veronica glanced at the books, as if she was resisting the urge to pick one up and start reading from it. "I've been thinking about this too—just exactly this: What's our realm of choice?

"Did you know?" she said, "that if you destroy a spider's web, it rebuilds from exactly the place it left off? It's like it has this program and it has to finish it, no matter what happens. Or like quantum physics."

She laughed at herself and glanced up at the corner of the room. "I know. I've been thinking too much. I sit in this little room and . . ." She waved her hand in front of her face, the way she had done at his house on Windy Creek. But then she went on, "The butterfly effect. The flap of a butterfly wing on this side of the world can cause a storm on the other side. Thomas Aquinas didn't know anything about that when he laid down the doctrine of free will for all time and eternity. I mean, the fact is that we don't even know what effect our actions have. We'll never see it; they might be subtle and small, as you say, but they also might be quite dramatic. You say it wouldn't have mattered what choices we made because everything that was controlling us was so much stronger than we were."

"That's not exactly what I was saying—"

"Okay, but let me finish. Isn't that just the thing? Don't we need integrity in our actions and to choose carefully because we don't know the effects?"

"Does the butterfly choose carefully? Does the spider? Does the butterfly have integrity?" He found he was reacting badly to that word, but he didn't know why. "You just said, the spider can't choose not to finish the web. It's compelled to finish what it started." He found himself speaking faster than he intended, with something even like anger.

She didn't reply. She didn't seem angry, just fiercely searching for something, reaching in and through the silence for an understanding. He wanted to give it to her, but he couldn't.

"So Hastings," she said finally, with a sigh, as if giving up momentarily on the search.

"Hastings."

"They want you to go."

"Are you saying that we should finish things even after they've lost purpose?" He wasn't ready to let it go. "Is that what integrity is?"

"I think what I'm saying is that a spider can't move on until the web is completed, that's all. It's not the product, I think," she said. "I think integrity is the process. The web is broken. That fact doesn't change. But still we've got something we have to do."

They didn't seem to have reached an end; maybe not even a beginning. Joe felt that everything that he had experienced since Veronica's visit in July was here in this conversation. Bear's predicament. Alice's demands. Vincent's haunting of them. The school. The letters. St. Rose. It was all here and floating around, trying to find a place in words like choice and integrity, effects, maybe even truth. But he felt like he couldn't even begin to tell her the story. He suddenly imagined walking with her down to the edge of Windy Creek in the spring and saying to her, "Look at how the ice turns into little islands as it melts."

"Hey," he said instead, looking up. "I've got kind of an errand to run. I could use some company." He stood up and looked around for a place to set his mug. She stood up too and took it from him. She looked at her watch and seemed to consider something.

"Sure," she said. "Let me get my coat."

21

Ice Islands

AS THEY HEADED across the frozen driveway, Joe instinctively reached out to hold her elbow. When they reached the Buick, he opened the door for her on the ditch side. He got in and started the car.

"Are you ready for an adventure?" he asked. She raised her lovely eyebrows and smiled.

They took the highway toward Sioux Falls. Between the heater and the sun, albeit already fading a little, the car felt almost warm. This time, Joe skirted the downtown. He drove toward the far west edge of the city, where he imagined the little girl waiting for him.

"I don't know if I really will go to Hastings," he said as they drove.

"Is that the kind of thing you can say no to?" she asked in a mild voice, as if it didn't frighten her to consider it, as it did him.

"Maybe that's what I was trying to ask you. Realm of choice and all that."

"It's always ulterior motives with you, Joseph," she said with a little laugh. It wasn't an accusation.

They pulled up in front of the school and joined a line of cars. The doors of the school opened, and children poured out the front, their coats and backpacks a mosaic of color against the white of the snow and yellow of the school. He opened the door and stood up so that the girl could see him. She came running toward them, swinging her backpack from one arm and then hoisting it up over her shoulder.

"You came!" she said.

"This is my friend, Mrs. Foster." Veronica had also gotten out of the car.

"Hello, Mrs. Foster," the girl said in that singsong formality that alternated with her exuberance. He had the feeling that strangers came and went in this child's life. He wondered if it was of any value to warn her about not accepting rides from them.

She climbed into the back seat, backpack first.

"That's for you," Father Joe said, gesturing toward the coat. "You should really have a coat in weather like this." He turned to Veronica as they got back in the car. "Mrs. Foster," he said, "I would like to introduce you to this person, but I don't know her name."

"Rowena," she said. "Rowena Campbell. For the town. Rowena. Where I was born."

"And where are we going, Rowena Campbell?"

"77334 State Highway 42."

They turned onto the highway and drove back in the direction from which both Father Joe and the girl had come. When they'd crossed the river, the girl said, "Here!" Father Joe didn't see anything, but he slowed.

"You missed it," she said. "There's a driveway. You can't really see it."

He backed up, and then he saw a steep road, rutted with tracks. As he turned to go down it, he wondered if the Buick would get back up it. The air temperature was dropping. It would only get icier. The road ended quickly at a small cluster of houses that no one would ever see from the highway.

"That one," Rowena said. She pointed to an old two-story

farmhouse with peeling paint and a sunken front porch. It looked like a relic of the nineteenth century. Parked in front was a rusty-paneled Oldsmobile that must be the car that had not started in the morning's cold. There was also a massive wood pile, like nothing he had ever seen. It was almost halfway up to the first story of the house and the width of a small parking lot. Whoever had chopped all of this wood had apparently foregone the formality of stacking it. Split logs were strewn everywhere. Snow drifted across the pile, burying some logs and exposing others. The man responsible, Joe finally discerned, was standing on the far side of the pile. He was wearing a turtleneck under a pair of denim overalls. A pair of work gloves was his only protection against the cold. He had red hair and gray stubble on his chin. He had glanced up briefly as they pulled in, but then went back to his work, using an old stump as a block for splitting and then tossing the split logs back toward the pile. The snow around him was laden with sawdust, as if he had been working for many hours.

Rowena opened the car door, and as she did, a woman appeared at the side of the house, coming up some steps from what looked like a basement. She was a small, slender woman with long, straight black hair. Father Joe's first impression was that she looked almost as young as Rowena. Perhaps a sister? But as she came closer, Joe could see the lines on her face and something of a roughness that he couldn't quite trace to a feature. He recognized it. He'd seen it often on Windy Creek. Hard living. Like Rowena, she was also not dressed to be outside. She didn't have socks on: bare ankles poked out of worn canvas tennis shoes.

When she emerged, the sound of chopping stopped briefly, as if the man who was chopping had noted her presence and wanted her to know. Then he'd returned to the rhythm of splitting and throwing.

The woman looked startled to see them, as if she had been in the dark all day and was now blinking into the light. She had one hand on her daughter's head, smoothing her hair.

"Are you social workers?" She squinted at them.

"No, we just . . . I ran into your daughter on my way into town this morning. From Windy Creek. She asked me for a ride home from school."

"Did you say Windy Creek? My grandmother lives there," the woman said distractedly, looking toward the man chopping wood. "I'm from there, I guess you could say." She folded her sweater more tightly around her in the wind. There was a certain elegance to her face, Father Joe noticed, a dreaminess that made him feel protective. "Starlotta Campbell."

"I don't think I know that name," Father Joe said.

"Well, if you're a priest, you wouldn't. She wasn't much of a churchgoer. You are a priest, right?" She was glancing at his black slacks and shoes.

He nodded in the dimming light. Her voice had the scratchiness of cigarette smoke and was deeper than he had expected.

"I almost forgot." He pulled the coat and snow pants, the mittens and hat, from the back seat. "These are for Rowena." The woman took them wordlessly. "It really was very cold this morning," he said, then regretted it. It sounded like scolding. Probably confirming everything this woman had ever thought about a priest.

Rowena had turned to go inside, but then suddenly ran back and threw her arms around Father Joe. He smelled the wood-smoke on her flannel shirt and in her hair before she released him and stood in front of Veronica more formally. "Thank you very much," she said.

Veronica laughed and kissed the top of the girl's head. "It was wonderful to meet you."

"Does this sort of thing happen to you often?" Veronica asked as they climbed the long, icy driveway slowly, with the Buick balking and occasionally spinning. The sky had turned lavender and a crescent moon had appeared, trailing Venus toward the western horizon.

"I don't leave the reservation often."

They reached the highway and started east again. Streetlights began to appear.

"How would that girl have made it home? In the dark, on the ice. That mother. What was she thinking?" Veronica wondered out loud and shivered. "Do you know that family? The Campbells?"

"Alice would," he said. "She would know whose cousin married which-who-from-where. I have trouble keeping track of things like that. She'd know three or four generations back and where they scattered to. Anybody who has ever had a grandmother on Windy Creek, I guarantee you Alice knows them or knows about them."

"Who's Alice?"

"Alice is . . ." He paused. Parishioner? Altar guild? Friend? "Alice is, I guess she's the reason I've survived on Windy Creek." Joe thought about repeating that so he could hear himself say it again. He'd never said it like that before.

"Isn't that strange?" Veronica said. "You leave Windy Creek this morning only to find Windy Creek waiting for you."

He hadn't escaped it at all. Windy Creek was everywhere, always, and it always would be. There was no driving away from it.

"I was trying to escape this morning," he said. "All of it. I wanted to be something, someone else for a few hours. But that didn't exactly work."

"Where are we going?" Veronica said.

"Aren't you . . ." He paused. "Expected?"

"Well, I don't know," she said. Streetlights moved through the car, illuminating them and dimming them at regular intervals. Snow piles gleamed and then were consumed by darkness.

At last, she said, "I say drive."

"Drive where?"

"Anywhere. Just go. Let's go somewhere where no one knows either of us."

He turned north and then east toward the Minnesota border. Minnesota was where they had met. Minnesota seemed like a place at a great distance—another civilization.

"Are you hungry?" he asked. "I know a steakhouse in Pipestone. Do you know anybody in Pipestone?"

"I don't think so."

The country was wide open here, evidence of habitation well hidden in groves of cottonwoods with tiny lights glimmering. Everything is concealed in this country. It's a paradox. It looks so exposed, all wind and sky, but the real stuff is hidden.

In that wide-open landscape, a car felt like a peculiar intimacy. Joe felt like he might say things into the darkness of the car that he had never said before to anyone. And whatever he said might disappear down the highway without consequence.

"What would it look like," she said, keeping her face turned out the windshield, "to say no to Hastings? Would you have to leave the priesthood? Could you ask for a reassignment?"

"I don't think I'd really thought about it at all until I said it to you a couple of hours ago." He might like to go back to the moment before he descended the cellar stairs, to the moment before that rubber band fell off of those old mimeographs. He could have gone on as before. Friend to the church. Friend to the people. One of the good guys. He was surprised to feel himself blinking back tears. When was the last time he'd cried? When was the last time he'd cried in the presence of another person?

He cleared this throat. "There are no words," he said.

"There are words, somewhere, I think," she said. "You just have to find them."

"Even if I found them, what would I do with them?"

"What you always do. Translate."

He reached across the space between them and took her hand. It accepted his touch. Her fingers were slightly cool, inordinately, unexpectedly soft. They drove forward into Minnesota, as if they'd been traveling through space and come upon a black hole, where all matter was irrelevant. It was a place where space and time dissolved except for this one little capsule hurtling forward into nothing, from nothing.

22

Night Driving

"WE'RE LOOKING for his mother, and it's almost like we've decided that if we find her, everything will be settled. But there is so much that still remains. Vincent is out there, somewhere, with maybe a vendetta. We don't know whether Bear will be tried as an adult. If there is a trial, where will it take place? Should he plead guilty or self-defense? Even if we find Bear's mother, the most likely scenario is still that he spends the rest of his adolescence in some juvenile detention center. But we can't bear to think about that, so we fixate on finding his mother."

The steakhouse lights were dim, and they sat in a leather corner booth, with a small candle flickering on the table. Steaks had been ordered. Salads had arrived: iceberg lettuce with too-thick slices of cucumber and a chunk of tomato or two with blue cheese dressing draped over them. Father Joe had a Scotch. Veronica had a glass of white wine.

In the dark-paneled room, there were only a few people out. Even so, Father Joe had looked around to make sure there was no one he knew.

"How much time have you got?" Veronica asked.

"April. The judge postponed the question of jurisdiction until

April. But Bear still has to do all of his check-ins with the court, and that makes me nervous. He hasn't exactly proven stable."

"I like this kid," Veronica said. "He strikes me as deep, the way you describe him. Fierce and thoughtful at the same time."

"I'd like to wring his neck."

The waitress brought steaks and potatoes. From the tray, she unloaded a glass dish of butter patties, each molded in the shape of a flower.

"Another?" She gestured toward his glass.

"Yes, thanks."

He turned back to Veronica and noticed the light dancing in her green eyes. It was amazing how lightly she took things, how she moved with ease through these decidedly awkward moments while he blustered and bumbled so clumsily. Maybe that's what you learned, being out in the world. How to improvise. How to take whatever comes. Whereas none of his much-practiced gestures were of any use here.

"I'm sorry, Joseph," she said, "but I feel like there is so much you aren't telling me. We've been trying to have a conversation for hours now, maybe our whole lives, and you dart around the subjects, hoping I'll be satisfied with little offerings. I'm not. I'm not satisfied. For example, what made you leave Windy Creek this morning?"

It was like he could smell the letters sitting on his desk, that slight acid scent of the ink, the must of them. The secret was not his. It belonged to the whole church. Did that mean that it also belonged to her? She was in the church, wasn't she? What if he told her—about Flynn, about Fabian, even about Brother Jerry? What if he told her what he saw, about the rot that went so deep that he hadn't yet seen the end of it? What happened next? He looked out at the darkness beyond the restaurant's window. He felt little drops of sweat along his hairline and on his nose. He picked up his napkin and wiped his face. The fireplace, the Scotch, the lack of sleep: it all snuck up on him. He felt dizzy. How would he make it home to Windy Creek in time for morning mass?

"Let me try this way," he said, shaking his head. "But I don't think it will be any better or any more satisfying. Once upon a time, there was a man whose life depended on keeping secrets. People told him everything. They told him about their anger, their crimes, their betrayals, the grudges they held. The times they wreaked vengeance. He ate secrets for breakfast, lunch, and dinner. He had secrets with his coffee and secrets with his Scotch." He held up his glass. He didn't know where this story would end.

"Eventually, there were two worlds. One made entirely of secrets, of which he could never speak. The other was the world where he lived like an ordinary person. Everybody who told him their secrets seemed to have no problem with him knowing, although they were a little formal with him, kept him at a distance. And he was pretty good at it. Keeping secrets. He kept them like boxes of junk. He would pronounce everyone forgiven, but they all still harbored the fear that he held on to it somewhere.

"But then one day, he found out there was a secret that no one had told him. It was a secret with the power to unmake the world. And that secret was not actually in someone else. It was inside him. But he had kept it even from himself."

He couldn't tell if Veronica was satisfied with this way of telling the story or if she was now more impatient than ever.

"Was the secret only in him or was it also out in the world?"

"What do you mean?" He wished he had a clear enough head to perceive what she was asking.

"I mean, did the secret have any effects in the world or did it only have effects inside this man?"

"It had many, many effects in the world. It was being lived out everywhere around him, all the time. He just hadn't been able to see it. And then one day, he could."

She nodded. That nod was the most comforting thing he had

ever seen. If there was one thing he could save from this whole day, from this whole evening, it would be that. The way she nodded, as if, even for an instant, she understood him. He didn't want to say one thing more. He wanted to leave it there, with that nod.

But then he went on. "The church is set up with the assumption that people come to it as penitents. They are sinners, those poor people, and the church comes along and offers them absolution, reconciliation. Everything we do revolves around that. Our catechism, the sacrament of reconciliation, preparation for the Eucharist, Eucharist itself. Of course, no one expects individual priests to be perfect, not to sin. They are part of the whole thing. They confess. They are offered absolution. It's all done under the dome of the church. But what if, what if the church is the sinner? To whom can it confess? Who can absolve?"

He saw what she meant about this not being satisfying. He was actually talking to avoid speaking. She would know this, of course. But meanwhile, he studied the lines on her face. He wanted to know what had made each one, what was her daily life and how had it come to reside on her face. He wanted to turn the conversation back to might-have-beens. But he couldn't find the words. She would ask "What was the church's sin?" And he would only have those haunting, horrible, fragmented words. *Panties. Basement. Nice talk.* How he hated them. How he didn't want them here between them.

But she didn't ask, as if she, even she, a fearless seeker to him, a person who wanted the truth and was willing to look for it, didn't want to know.

The ride back was quieter than Joe wanted. Veronica seemed preoccupied. Joe was still trying out various versions of his story in his head, wondering if there still might be one he could offer, even as the moment had passed.

Around Jasper, Joe spoke. "I heard a creation story once. I can't remember whose story it was. It's about the first Earth Daughter who went outside to shake her sleeping blanket. Each particle of dust flew up into the sky and became a bird. And each bird flew high enough to become a star. That's how we got this blanket of stars. Now we wait for each star bird to return to the earth, one at a time."

"That's beautiful," Veronica said, a little sleepily. "Are you going to see that little girl again?"

"I don't know."

"Something feels unfinished about that, doesn't it?"

"It does. I almost feel like I should sleep by the side of the road so I can pick her up again tomorrow and take her to school. But maybe this time, she at least has a coat. I feel like I helped her for one day, but the problem goes on and on. Unsatisfying." He borrowed her word.

The night flowed along outside.

"There is something I have always wanted, something that I can't have and still be a priest," he said. "Maybe it makes no difference, but once I say it, I can't unsay it."

"Joseph, what is it?"

"I'd like to spend one whole night with you. Just one night. It doesn't have to be more than one. I don't have to even touch you. But I want that intimacy. The dark-to-dawn knowing. Of you."

She didn't answer. The quiet made him burn with shame. "Ridiculous," the voice said.

"Do you remember the first time you touched me?" she asked. She raised her hand to her cheek.

"I do."

"No one has ever touched me like that since."

He dropped Veronica off at her driveway. He could see the lights from the living room through the blinds, making streaks on the snowy front lawn. He watched her walk to the front door, with her hood up over her head and her purse on her shoulder. He felt an ache as she opened the door and disappeared behind it. He imagined the man waiting for her on the other side, this Darel. Then he turned the car around on the gravel and began the long drive back to Windy Creek.

23

Love Shelter

"CAMPBELL?" Alice and Father Joe were in the chapel. Before he had gone to bed the previous night, arriving in the frozen dark, he had gone into the church and replaced the hawk feather exactly as he had left it. He had no idea if she had noticed its disappearance or its replacement. Eventually, he would ask her and maybe, he thought, he would try to account for all the other silences and missteps and evasions of his life at the same time.

Now she was filling the candleholders with oil and preparing the Advent wreath. Father Joe sat in the front pew telling her about his adventures in Sioux Falls.

"That Campbell woman was mean. Mean," she said. "The girls, they scattered like ragweed. They got out of there as fast as they could."

"She had daughters?"

"She had a whole mess of daughters. Maybe five or six of them. She stayed out there by herself and lived mean. So this woman you met, she said she had a grandmother called Campbell? What did the woman look like?"

"She was small, sharp."

"That'd be her. The Campbells were all small. They were like those blackbirds that chase after hawks—smart, quick—sharp beaks."

"She also had a daughter, a really extraordinary little girl. She's the one I saw first, walking to school in the bitter cold on the road. An old soul. She didn't have that same look as her mother. I couldn't get over how different the two of them looked from each other. But they were almost the same size."

"How old was she?"

"The daughter?"

"The mother." Alice was calculating, Father Joe could see, bringing this new information into the web of the old, trying to see where the pieces fit.

"Maybe thirty? Old enough to have lived hard. The daughter was nine or ten, something like that."

"Campbell," Alice repeated to herself, like some bell had gone off at a distance and she was trying to hear it. "I haven't thought about them in years. I wonder if their house is still out there by Ghost Lake. I should take a walk over there one of these days and see."

The holidays were coming upon them fast now. No one in the tribe or the state or law enforcement was particularly interested in moving things along with Bear's case. Even the lawyer was silent. Bear stayed close to Alice, like he was watching out for her. Every once in a while he went up to Gayle's to check on the old man. Father Joe wondered if they talked about dreams. He pictured them by the woodstove, working on the saddles. He wondered what would happen if he told them the dream about losing at poker or finding the man in the sea. He remembered the sound of their voices behind the closed door and wished he could be in the room.

Father Joe wondered if he could file a complaint to the police department in Rapid City about the night that Albert died. They should know that they have racist cops in that department, maybe even a murderer. But he imagined calling them up and reporting what Bear had said Vincent had said. It wasn't going to work. Why would they listen? Was anyone even investigating Albert's death? They hadn't heard from the Rapid City police in ages. Not one single detective had ever asked them a question, as far as he knew.

A Christmas card arrived from Veronica. There was a brightly colored holiday stamp in the corner of the green, glossy envelope. He didn't open it. The last thing he could imagine wanting from her was some kind of stilted, falsely cheerful greeting, as if the night in the car hadn't happened. And if she'd signed it "Veronica and Darel" or "Merry Christmas from the Fosters!," then he thought he might die from the penmanship.

Father Joe had never understood why people sat down with a box of cards and signed them out one by one to friends and family with nothing more than a signature at the bottom. It had never made any sense to him. He knew he should do this as part of St. Rose outreach, but he never had been able to force himself into it. What was the transaction in that ritual? It bothered him that Veronica was now including him in her version. He didn't want to be on her Christmas card list.

He went through the rituals of Christmas as if in a trance. He still didn't tell the people of St. Rose that this was their last Christmas together, and that made him feel like a traitor.

Then January brought a shift. Even though the temperatures were colder than ever, it felt like Windy Creek had been rediscovered by the sun. The light became starker and cast sharper shadows. There were more cloudless days, however cold. Father Joe called it "Winter. Act II."

Father Joe had moved the letters to the bookshelf and put a paperweight on top of them. He'd left them open. This felt like a tepid form of courage. Someone, anyone could walk into his office and read them if they wanted to. He felt a bit like he was airing them out. Every time he looked at them, he felt their personal poison diminish slightly. Something was growing in him, however subtle. His *leb*—he thought. The psalmist's word for heart. Two letters: Lamed. Lamed signified love, wonder, and learning. And Bet, which looked like a little house, signified shelter. The heart was the love shelter, he translated, or the house of wonder. The heart was the place where inner guidance came from.

The heart was a secret part of the self, where something like truth is whispered, and if we can't hear it, if it's too noisy in there or if we've emptied it out too much or not been very good on the maintenance end of things, then we get lost. Something in us becomes shachath. A lot of translations used "corrupt" for this word, but Father Joe felt the Hebrew was stronger, and now he saw it as connected to the delicate love shelter: it caves in.

Could it be rebuilt—that leb? St. Rose was Father Joe's little love shelter, his house of wonder. His place to come in from the ru'ach—the wind, the storm, the tempest. It was soon to become shachath. He thought of Veronica's spiderweb that has been half-ruined by an unknown hand. He thought of the web that Alice built in her mind that seemed to connect everyone and everything together.

Let me fly away from all of this. Give me wings like the dove. That is how I would find rest. That's how the psalms expressed it. It's a wish. Hadn't Joe discovered that Windy Creek was everywhere? There was no flying away. But he could feel that ache again, that longing to drive and drive, somewhere, anywhere. The ocean? *Oh, to have wings like the dove.* To be human is to always be forgetting, forgetting and forgetting at every moment that you are one tiny thread in a vast work not of your own making.

———

At the end of January, Alice knocked at the open office door.

"Father, do you have a minute?"

She sat on the couch and couldn't help but take a quick swipe at the dust on the coffee table. He thought she was going to pull out a handkerchief from her purse, but she stopped, as if catching herself in the act.

"We need to go see that Campbell girl you found."

She let that sink in and then continued. "She would have been at the school at the same time as Bear's mother—if we are right that Bear's mother was at the school. This girl, the mother, whoever she was, she was not connected. She was not known. Her story was kept apart. So we've got to look to the margins. The Campbells are nothing if not on the margins.

"I can't shake the feeling that all of this is tied up with Bear's dream. I'm sorry, Father. I know you aren't much one for dreams and what they mean. But I think we've got to go and check it out."

"When?"

"Tomorrow. After mass. You drive."

"Is Bear going?"

"We need him. I am going to prepare him, because he needs to be ready to tell us about the road."

"Can he even do that? Leave the reservation?"

"Well, we aren't exactly going to be telling anyone, are we?"

She went to the door and then turned back.

"Thank you," she said.

He looked up and met her eyes. They were deep and soft, velvety, and he felt like he could fall into them and stay forever.

24

Red Rock Valley

THAT EVENING he picked up Veronica's card from where it had sat next to the phone for weeks. "There's no harm in it," he told himself. "It's just a Christmas card. It won't bite."

He sat with it in his hands at the kitchen table with his glass of Scotch, ice cubes melting and cracking. He felt the familiar weight of cardstock and looked at the slightly messy loops of her handwriting on the envelope, which always stirred him. "Opening an envelope should not be this hard," he thought. "You are making this out to be something when it is really nothing." Since their evening together, he wondered if Veronica was retreating from him at an irrecoverable distance. He wouldn't blame her. All his awkwardness and missteps. She probably felt she was trying to dance with a bear in the circus.

The card was what he'd expected: simple, elegant. A holiday greeting. But instead of the signature he'd dreaded, a letter fell out. It was folded into small pieces, a little island of white amid the green. When he unfolded it with the sense that he was finding a secret message, he saw that the handwriting was smaller and more compressed than Veronica's ordinary gait. She'd written this weeks ago, he thought, letting the Scotch burn his throat.

Dear Joseph,

If you are looking for my forgiveness, you have it. I absolve you. Once and for all. You are not under my judgment. I see now that our choices were inevitable, however much we might have questioned them at the time and since. No one is to blame for them. If you weren't Darel, I would have made you into Darel, because that was the choice I needed to make. If you'd married me instead of becoming a priest, you would have made yourself into a priest anyway because that was the choice you needed to make. There's mystery in that.

Meanwhile, I see that I have another choice in front of me. I can stay here and stew in my own mind, my own questions. Or I can go. I know that I need to go in search of my own life. I guess it's what the young people call finding yourself. I suppose I have a case of arrested development. It feels so adolescent. But I have to do it.

I will leave after the holidays, once the tree is packed up and I've stored all the leftovers in the freezer. The children will be back in their own lives. I know I have many nights ahead of me worrying about the consequences of what I am about to do. But there is no road without consequences.

I don't know where I am going. And you'll laugh at this: I don't know how many books to take with me. I think I'll take all of them. A lady with a roving library. A roving lady with a library.

I hope you don't think I am taking this lightly. It's the least well-thought-out thing I've ever done, but it isn't light. I know the pain I'm causing. Well, maybe not causing. Stirring up.

So look for word of me from the road somewhere. When I have a better idea of it, I'll let you know.

Veronica

He should have known, he thought. There was always more to Veronica than met the eye. At that moment, something in him shifted. He was listening far away.

The next morning, Father Joe pulled into Alice's driveway. Alice and Bear came out of the house with Marlena, who stood on the porch with her arms across her solid body, as if to say, "Mom, what are you doing?" Duty-bound Marlena. She was always there, doing what needed to be done. Carrying them all forward. He imagined extracting her from the web like a fly caught in silky threads, but then he understood, maybe for the first time, that extracting her would kill her. This was what she did. How had Veronica put it? We have these choices that we simply have to make. Here was Marlena's.

Alice had brought snacks: apples, jerky, a loaf of Wonder Bread, and her own wild grape jelly. She carried all of this in a cardboard box and set it on the seat between them. Then from her purse, she drew out the hawk feather. She had attached it to a leather cord and she hung this from the Buick's rearview mirror.

"What's the feather for?" Father Joe asked nonchalantly.

"It's a lot of things," Alice said. "It's a prayer. We're asking to see better, maybe to see something that isn't obvious."

They pulled out onto the highway. The road was clear, but the sun was blocked by a low bank of clouds.

"Have you thought any about what we are going to say to the Campbell girl when we find her?"

"No," she said with a sly glance in his direction. "I thought I'd let the Lord lead me."

"Oh, really? That's not like you. You are usually a good ways ahead and trying to get the Lord to catch up."

"Is that how it is?" She smiled. "He is slow. You have to admit."

———

Bear was quiet as they drove toward the great river. He had the silence of a sentinel. Watchful, alert, careful. Whatever preparation Alice had offered him, he was absorbed by it. Father Joe occasionally glanced at him in the mirror and studied his face. There was a skim of dark hair on his upper lip, a few pimples along his cheekbones.

The roads were clear, with mounds of dirty snow piled along the sides. Little marked Windy Creek off from the rest of South Dakota, and yet Father Joe felt a sharp tension, as if the stakes rose somehow as they left it. For Alice, certainly. For Bear.

They reached the outskirts of Sioux Falls by late morning, but it wasn't as easy to find Rowena's little road as Father Joe had imagined it would be. There were several gravel roads heading down from the highway, and Father Joe made a couple of unsuccessful tries, looking for the woodpile and the circle of homes. He even thought, briefly, that maybe he'd imagined the whole thing. Maybe there was no woodpile, no Campbell girl, no red-haired man with an ax. It all had a very dreamlike quality now. Finally, however, they descended the right road and pulled up in front of the woodpile. The same man with the beard was chopping wood, as if he had never left. But the Oldsmobile was nowhere to be found.

Father Joe turned off the engine, and all three of them got out of the car. The man with the ax stopped his relentless motion to stare at them with distinct hostility.

Father Joe made the first try. "Hello," he said. "We're looking for the woman who lives downstairs. Campbell? Her name is Campbell."

"Sally. Yeah. Well. She ain't here."

"Do you know where she is?"

He focused his ice-chip-blue eyes on Father Joe, then on Alice, and finally on Bear, where they lingered.

"Nope." He made a move like he was going to start chopping again.

"Do you have any idea when she'll be coming back?"

"She ain't coming back. Not if I have anything to say about it.

I kicked her ass out of here a week ago." He picked up a log and threw it toward the pile. Then he set another log on the stump and sent the ax through it with a satisfying *thunk*.

Father Joe looked at Alice. She shrugged. "I see," Father Joe said. "Thanks for your time."

The man didn't appear to respond.

When they reached the highway, Father Joe pulled the car over.

"What do we do?"

Alice turned to Bear. "What do we do now?" she asked.

He was quiet for a minute. Then he said, "You said she had a car? It was broke down?"

"Yes."

"Let's go into town. She can't be far away."

Father Joe said, "I don't know if you realize this, Bear, but that town is pretty big."

He shrugged.

They drove into town. Father Joe decided that maybe downtown was their best bet, avoiding the major arteries and the shopping malls. There was a soup kitchen downtown, the Salvation Army, a Union Gospel Mission. The streets were close together. There were alleys, unlike in the wide-open sprawl of the newer parts of town. If Rowena and her mother were homeless, it might be the best place. He parked the car on the far edge of downtown where there was a diner.

"Let's at least start here with something to eat," he said. The diner was a grimy little place, and the man behind the counter smoked while he made their burgers and fries. He was gray and slightly stooped, wearing a T-shirt and striped pants. He watched them, as if they were a spectacle to him, his only entertainment for the day and perhaps also some kind of threat. Father Joe wondered if they somehow had "reservation" stamped on them.

"What have you been thinking about Hastings, Father? You going?" Alice asked while they ate.

"I haven't gotten the details yet. I can't get my mind around it." He didn't tell her about the strange letter from Veronica, but still somehow it was there with them. He wondered if her experiment was already over and she was a few miles from here, returned to Darel and her meadow. Or if she was very far from here. California maybe, or Tennessee. He tried to think of random places a "roving lady" might go.

"Nebraska." Alice shuddered a little and looked around. "Is it a city, like this?"

"I think it's smaller. Close to Lincoln."

After lunch they decided to walk the downtown block by block. The car was blue, Father Joe told them. An Oldsmobile in bad shape. Rusted panels. The thing should look like it's unlikely to move.

A meager winter sunlight hit the sidewalks. Dirty snow was piled up on the curbsides. They walked by an old movie theater and a liquor store, a department store that looked like it had seen better days.

"What's that smell?" Bear asked as they walked.

"Meatpacking," Father Joe said. "There's a big plant up there." He gestured north, finding it odd that he was becoming the tour guide for a Sioux Falls he only barely knew. Yet they knew it less, he realized. Alice had gone into a fog. That smoky look she'd had after Albert's death had returned to her eyes. She was quiet. He remembered that she had a brother who'd done time in the penitentiary here, and that she used to come home from visiting him with something she called "river sick." Sioux Falls, for her, was a place where only the despairing went. You came here when you lost your connection, when you gave up on Windy Creek and the demands the land made.

They peered down side streets and into parking lots. Much of the downtown felt deserted, with empty storefronts and boarded-up windows. What could happen in a week? He wondered. Where would someone like Rowena's mother go?

After a few blocks, Bear stopped and pointed. They had reached one edge of downtown, where they were a block from the Big Sioux River. There was a bridge and, just before the bridge, a desolate stretch of pavement. Parked there was a blue, rusted Oldsmobile.

"Geez. Good eye, Bear," Father Joe said as they walked toward it. They peered in the window, where they could see a jumble of blankets and pillows, garbage sacks of what looked like clothing. "Bingo."

The place where the car was parked was a kind of no-man's-land. Even though it was a block off the main street, it had the feeling of being no place at all. There was one building, which appeared to be an abandoned manufacturing building of some kind with broken windows and crumbling brick.

They walked past the car onto the bridge and stood looking down at the water of the Big Sioux with its curlicues of ice and blue chunks like frosted glass. The air had the heavy, thick smell of animal death, something at once sweet and horrible. Fetid, but the mysterious part was that it was somehow bearable, carried on the wind from the north, filtering into everything, through everything.

"We've got to stake out the car," Bear said. He looked around, surveying the eastern bank of the river and beyond, where there was a neighborhood of clapboard houses with small porches and peeling paint.

"Isn't it a bit cold?" Father Joe said.

Bear narrowed his eyes and shoved his hands deeper into his pockets. He shrugged his distinctive shrug.

"We didn't come all this way for nothing."

"We'll take turns," Father Joe said. "Your mom and I will wait somewhere warm. Then we'll come back. You'll go warm up. And we'll keep trading until something happens or it gets dark. Deal?"

He nodded and trotted over to the rotting front porch of the manufacturing building. He jumped up and down a few times and then rubbed his hands together and blew on them.

"You want my hat?" Joe called.

He shook his head.

Father Joe and Alice turned back. Alice glanced behind. "I don't like leaving him there like that."

They walked back to the main street and looked around. There was a small coffee shop that was empty at this time of day, a plain place with plastic booths and a few tables, one man behind the counter who glanced up indifferently when they walked in.

"Would you drink a coffee?" Father Joe asked.

"Maybe just to keep my hands warm," she said.

They settled on stools at a counter facing the street, with their coffee in small, mottled mugs made of heavy plastic, and stared out on the ever-more gray and blue street.

"You hate it here," Father Joe said to Alice.

"How did you know?"

"The Alice I know left somehow, just about the time we turned onto Twelfth Street by the YMCA."

"Do you know about the rock, Father?"

"What rock?"

"The rock that this whole town is made out of? The whites call it Sioux Quartzite, and they built everything out of it: the courthouse and a museum and the high school. Even the penitentiary. But for us that rock is sacred. It has the blood of our ancestors in it. It's the rock that protects pipestone—the most sacred rock in the world. When I am here, all I can think about is all that blood. It's almost like I can hear them crying." She shivered and looked out into the nearing dark.

"You are going to leave us," she said finally, as if pulling herself awake and shaking something off.

"I don't think I have a choice."

"I don't know, Father, how you are going to make it with all those wasichun."

"You know, when I came to Windy Creek, you didn't think I was going to make it among the Indians."

"I know, I know," she said with a little smile, and turned toward him. "But I was wrong about you. You've got a little of Windy Creek in you now. Think about it. You know how to find lost things. You know how to read the land—at least a little. It's different. You're different."

"I did find something," Father Joe said heavily. He hadn't practiced this conversation in his head. Every time he thought about telling Alice about the letters, he swerved around it mentally. He couldn't find an opening.

"When I was looking through the guest books," he began, "I found some letters. I never should have had those letters. But I took them, a long time ago. I never read them until we were looking for Bear's mother."

She looked at him sharply.

"They are letters from Bernard Fabian. Do you remember him? He used to run Blessed Sacrament when it was a school?"

Alice snorted. "I remember him. He thought he should have been given an appointment at the Vatican and he ends up on the rez in South Dakota, wiping snot from Indian kids' noses. Yes. I remember him.

"Wait," she said. "Bernard. Bernard Fabian. I never thought about where Bear's mother would've gotten that name. Do you think he could be? When was he at Blessed Sacrament?"

"The timing is right," Father Joe said, feeling like they had skirted the main thing.

Alice said, "We should have been looking for Bernards all along. Do you think he's Bear's father? That he got a girl at the school pregnant and then erased all records of her?"

Father Joe tried to think about the man he had known. His efficiency. The fussiness of his style. He tried to probe the realm of secrets, but he came up empty. In the letters, Fabian had joked about running off with Louise Francis, a devout Catholic woman with ten kids. In truth, he realized, he didn't know anything about how Fabian handled the chastity part of his vows. Nothing at all. He'd assumed the man was too obsessed with power to think about things of the body. He tried to imagine if he saw any part of Fabian in Bear—the thought made him shudder—but he also felt like sight wasn't sufficient. Something else was needed, and it wasn't found in memory or in guessing.

Alice was still mulling this over. "Those girls. They had a pretty vicious sense of humor," she said. "I mean, it could also have been a poke in the eye at him. He wouldn't have to be the actual father for a girl to want to point a finger at him."

"Because?"

"There's so much that went on at that school, Father." He waited to see if she wanted to say more. Alice brought her mug to her lips and then, as though she couldn't bring herself to swallow the liquid, set it back down on the counter.

"I know," he said in almost a whisper. He was looking down, his cheeks hot.

"It wasn't every priest," she said. "You knew which ones. We always said they sent the bad ones to us. There were certain ones. They'd get this look. You learned to read it. Some girls ran away. Some girls thought they were clever enough to avoid it. Some fought—fists and everything. Your skin had this prickly feeling the whole time. It wasn't just girls.

"The nuns always told us we were the ones who were dirty. We were the ones who had sin. They always told us how they admired the priests, and we should look up to them.

"Sometimes, inside, it was like a tornado siren, like this horrible ringing in your ears. But it was also so normal. Just how things were. Like you might get used to a siren if it was going off all the time, learn to live with it. It was easier to believe you were bad than to try to figure out why nothing was the way it should be. I mean, that's what it was like when I was there. And even if you knew something was wrong, who could you tell? Who would listen to you?

"Some of the girls drank. Some hurt themselves. Some of us—we buried everything. Blood and fights and alcohol—all of that was more real than what they said at the school.

"It's hard on people," she said. "When you have these different truths. One has all the power. The other one seems to have all the pain, and you can't trust what you see with your own eyes, hear with your own ears."

While she spoke, her eyes were focused on some point out on the ice-crusted street, with the blackish mounds of plowed snow. Father Joe dared a glance at her profile. Her narrow nose and full lips, the graceful lift of her cheekbones.

"I don't have any words for it, Alice."

"We need to find some, don't we?" She sat up straighter in her wool coat. This was what Veronica had said. That there was the possibility of looking for words, even when you didn't have them.

"None of us can change what we are given to live," she said. "But if you think a single day goes by where I don't wish I could give my children something better. . . . There are no days like that."

"Are we? Are we giving them something better?" He hated that he was looking to her for some kind of reassurance.

She studied him and let the question hang. "You go check on Bear," she said. "I don't like him out there by himself. Trade with him and send him back here."

25

Crow Bar

THE AFTERNOON was quickening toward dusk, and Father Joe could tell that it was going to snow. He saw Bear ahead of him on the steps of the building.

"Any action?" Father Joe said.

"None."

"Go keep your mom company," Father Joe said. "Here's five bucks. For a Coke or whatever."

He smiled. He seemed emboldened by his shift. Cold but energized, as if he'd found some hidden fuel in his work. Father Joe didn't feel the same. He bounced up and down a little in his shoes and stamped back and forth. He started counting minutes.

But it wasn't long before Bear came running toward him.

"She's not there!"

"What do you mean?"

"It's that coffee place, right? On the corner? There's no one there."

Father Joe struggled to keep pace with Bear as they ran back to the main street. The stool where he had left Alice was empty. The two of them paused, bewildered and disoriented.

"Okay," Bear said. "We have to split up. I'll go to the car because I know what I'm looking for. You gotta look around." He studied the street. "Here."

"Half an hour. Meet at the car, Okay?" Father Joe said. "I don't want to lose you too."

Bear turned and ran back toward the bridge.

Father Joe stood in front of the café and looked in every direction. The street was all but empty. A few people passed by with their collars turned up against the cold. In the dimming light, shapes began to take on dimension. Was that a person? No, just the lump of a fire hydrant. Was that something moving? No, just the shimmering uncertainty of dusk. Cars with headlights occasionally sent up slush, showering the street with light that then receded. He hesitated to walk from here. Alice obviously knew where he would be, but where would she have gone?

Two shapes gradually emerged from the north. He squinted at them, waiting for them to disappear like another mirage. He dared not move in case motion would scare them away.

"Alice!" He waved. With her was, unmistakably, Rowena. The same hitch of the backpack, the same thrift store pants, but she was wearing the jacket and the hat that he had bought, and he felt relief in that.

"How did you . . . ?"

"I was waiting for Bear when I saw this little girl walk by. She looked just like you'd described her, and I thought she might even be heading for the car. But I followed her to the library."

"I go there every day," Rowena said.

"I asked if she remembered you."

"I did!" said Rowena. Alice smiled.

"This isn't the same lady you were with before," Rowena said.

Alice lifted her eyebrows and looked in Joe's direction.

"No," he said. "No, this is a different one."

"This one is nice too."

"Where's your mother?" Father Joe said.

"She always meets me at the library when it closes."

"But where is she?"

The girl shrugged. "Sometimes she's at the Crow Bar. Sometimes at O'Reilly's. She likes the gambling machines at Dillenger's. It's okay. She won't notice I'm not at the library until later."

With the dark came a light snowfall. They turned toward the bridge and the car, where Bear was waiting.

He was standing under the lone streetlamp that had come on at dusk with a light snow falling around him. He was dancing. It took Father Joe a moment to recognize it. He was dancing in a circle as if at a powwow, in a simple step-hop. He was concentrating deeply, maybe even praying. Father Joe felt a panic. He imagined a police car coming by. The neighbors calling. Bear knew so little about cities, about the eyes that can be watching you, about how people huddle into their own solitary lives and protect themselves. Bear, despite everything, had not learned self-protection. But there were no neighbors here, and the street was empty and silent.

"Who's that?" Rowena asked.

"That's my son," Alice answered.

Rowena sprinted ahead of us and ran until she was two feet from Bear. She stopped and stood absolutely still. He stopped as well and turned toward her. Joe and Alice instinctively slowed their steps.

As they got closer, they heard Bear say, "Are you the one we've been looking for?" But they couldn't hear Rowena's reply.

———

When they all stood together under the streetlamp, Alice took the lead. "We've got to find Rowena's mother and we've got to take them to Windy Creek. That's all there is to it. We can't have them living in this car."

Father Joe turned to Rowena. "Do you know where the Crow Bar is?"

"Yes." She sounded skeptical. "Father Joe, do you think we could eat a grilled cheese sandwich? They had corn dogs and Jell-O for lunch today at school, and it was kinda gross."

The lights of the diner shone onto the street. They found a booth, and the same man with his dirty apron and striped pants brought them menus. He pretended that he didn't recognize them, even though it had only been a few hours since they had last sat here. He must be the only employee. Or owner. Cook, waiter, the whole business. The place was called the Nickel Plate, and Father Joe wondered when it had been that you could get a plate for a nickel. That must have been a long time ago. The man had an agelessness about him. Maybe he was here then.

He brought them sandwiches, and they ate, as if already a companionable family, two grandparents with two children, the only customers.

"What do you think of this idea of Windy Creek, Rowena?" Father Joe asked.

"I don't know what that is. Is it a place?"

"It's a safe place," Alice said.

"Is it far away?"

"It's pretty far away," Father Joe said. "We'd have to drive there, and it would take a little while."

Rowena shook her head vigorously. "Nope. We can't leave the car."

"Why not?" Father Joe asked.

"It's the only thing we have, and we can't lose it. That's why. And it's helped us a lot. Like when Axel kicked us out and we even got it up the hill from his place. That was a true miracle." She said the words again as if she liked them, this time drawing them out. "True miracle."

"Let's start by finding your mom. Then we'll worry about the rest of it," Father Joe said. Alice stayed quiet. He could tell that her mind was already made up. There wasn't even a real question. They would all sleep that night in Windy Creek, one way or another. They would get away from this place where you could hear the ancestors crying as fast as possible. They would take Rowena and her mother with them. That was final. That was how it would be done, and it didn't require any more argument or discussion. It was the same certainty he had known in her since she had decided that Bear was "one of ours." He was glad to feel it again, even here. He knew that he relied on it.

The Crow Bar was at the other end of downtown, in the direction they had come and not far from the library where Rowena had been headed when Alice had seen her and rightly guessed who she was. Father Joe and Alice left Rowena and Bear in the back seat of the Buick and went together toward the neon sign that flashed red onto the street in front of the bar. The sign had a crow on it, dressed in a top hat and a red waistcoat, peering down at them, a sinister guardian, as they opened the door to the bar.

The bar was dark and their eyes took a moment to adjust. There were only a few people scattered around—a few at the bar itself and a few at the back playing pool. At first it seemed unlikely that they would find the "Campbell girl" here. But gradually their eyes adjusted through the dim light and the smoke, and they saw her. She was in the far corner, on the other side of the pool table between the back door and the jukebox. She was dancing, as though alone, and it was a strange thing to take in from where they stood. Her dancing was the opposite of Bear's earlier intense concentration—that focus of limb and mind. This was all loose and fluid, all liquid. She was small and fragile; it was like watching a flower wilt in fast-forward. She was dressed in jeans and a short-cropped T-shirt, and it was obvious that she was drunk. They also saw that there was a man, in the farthest booth, in a cowboy hat, watching her. It was even possible that they were together, Father Joe thought as he and Alice stared awkwardly in the woman's direction.

Alice and Joe's entrance had attracted the attention of everyone in the bar, except the woman who was dancing. Father Joe looked the bartender in the eye and nodded.

"Can I help you?" the bartender said. He was a young man with heavy jowls and a wary smile.

"We are looking for someone," Father Joe said. He gestured with his head toward the back of the bar.

"Sally?" The bartender raised his eyebrows and stared at Father Joe's collar. "She's here," he said a little wearily. "She's always here."

Father Joe and Alice walked together toward the back. Father Joe cleared his throat. "Sally. Sally Campbell."

The woman did not stop dancing immediately. She slowed her circling as if she were responding to an inner music.

"What do you want?" She stumbled a little and then stopped. The man who had been watching her got up from the booth and ordered another drink. Then he turned and leaned against the bar, watching them.

"Is something wrong? Is it Rowena? She's at the library. She's fine. You're not reporting me." The thought of Rowena had awakened her a little, and she narrowed her eyes, trying to steady herself.

"Could we sit down a minute?" Alice asked.

She let them lead her toward a booth. Alice folded her hands on the table and leaned toward the other woman. Father Joe felt like he was too bulky a presence for this delicate conversation between the two women. He wondered if he should get up and go to the bathroom or order them a drink or go check on the kids in the car. But he stayed, imagining his body as a kind of shield.

"I need your help," Alice started. Sally was having trouble focusing. "Sally, I'm Alice Nighthawk. I'm Winona Nighthawk's daughter. Do you remember? You knew my son Albert."

She shook her head. "If you need my help, buy me a drink," she said.

"It's a long story," Alice said. "But I wonder if I could take you to my house. I've got beds you could sleep on. I can tell you the whole story in the morning."

"Where d'you live?" She considered the offer for a moment, balancing her desire to be rid of them against her need.

"Windy Creek," Alice said.

"No way. I'm not going there." She glanced longingly toward the bar and the man who had a drink waiting for her.

"I can help you," Alice said.

"You know what." She stared at them across the table. "Just get the hell out of here. I don't care what you need. This is none of your goddamn business."

Father Joe and Alice exchanged glances. "Get the fuck out," she said, as if trying to make it final. She raised her voice enough that the man at the bar had started to move in their direction. She got out of the booth with some effort and went to join him. They started dancing.

Alice and Father Joe stared at the empty place she had left. The woman's eyes stayed on them as they made their way to the door and out onto the snowy street.

"What now?" Father Joe asked.

"I guess we wait for her at the library. Maybe she'll be a little more sober by then."

"Right," Father Joe said. "We should report this." Alice gave him a look. Not a look. *The* look. The Alice look. God, he would miss it. Would anyone look at him like that in Hastings? They wouldn't. It would be all deference and politeness and jockeying for position around him. That's how it was in churches.

The library's interior was warm and well lit. Past the librarian's cautious eye, Rowena led them to the children's section.

"This is my table. This is what I'm reading." She had gone to a shelf and picked up a book that she handed to Bear. Father Joe glanced at the title, *The Mouse and the Motorcycle.* "I'm on page thirteen," she said directly to Bear. "Read to me."

The hour passed with Father Joe and Alice deep in thought on their own sides of the table, and Bear reading aloud in a voice that had turned deep in only the last few weeks. Here he was, reading with an almost man's voice, about a mouse named Ralph, in his long-limbed, almost-man's body, and yet no time had passed at all since he was a child. Would they ever go fishing again? Would they ever look for feathers or arrowheads together? Already he could feel Bear moving away from him.

What was the word that they used for Flynn's sins? In Minnesota, Rossling had used the word "misconduct." Misconduct could cover a multitude of things in the most benign fashion possible. "Misconduct" was a word you could say in public. What were the words you could not say? He had to find the words they could not say, not the ones they already had in hand. Those were the words that they'd used to effectively manage the situation.

Molester. That word contained the darkness that Father Joe was looking for. *Child molester.* Even in all these years, he had not said those words to himself. He'd said "bad news." What had he said to Fabian—"bad business"? That had had no effect, he recalled, except to raise the man's ire. But he had never said "molester." But wasn't it a mistake to think that one word, the right word, the appropriate word, would matter? He had already started composing a letter to the bishop in his head. Could he use the word "molester" in the letter? Would that finally wake them up? Shake loose whatever was frozen in them?

Surely God will bring you to everlasting ruin. He will snatch you up and pluck you from the tent.

Truth was something that stole upon you, a sneak. Sometimes it took years for it to find the light. It crept around, one step out of the way for years and years, hovering in the darkness, not willing to say its name. But wasn't truth light? Wasn't it supposed to be light? How could it hover in darkness like a jackal? Truth hovered in the filing cabinet of the vicar general's office, in the basement in cardboard boxes. If you wanted to find it, you'd go there. But who ever wanted to find it?

"The library will be closing in ten minutes," a female voice said over the intercom. They looked at each other, somewhat helplessly. There was no Sally. Outside, in the falling snow, there was still only darkness and Rowena's scowl. Father Joe could feel how quietly and yet how desperately the girl was working to make this all right, to show them that she and her mother were fine, and this was all part of the normal go of things. Not a reason to worry. Not a reason to panic. Not a reason to call Social Services. He wondered how many times Child Protective Services had been called. How many encounters had this child had with social workers? She'd obviously learned a nonchalant posture to fend them off. She was determined to let them know that this was all okay.

Father Joe proposed they drive slowly back to the Crow Bar, in case Sally was on her way and running late. They drove slowly the few blocks, circling until they were convinced there was no one who resembled Sally on any of the streets. They drove back to the library parking lot in case they had missed her. Finally, at last, they parked in front of the Crow. This time Father Joe went in alone. The bartender was drying glasses.

"That woman . . . Sally." He remembered that the bartender had known her name.

"She left a while ago. Went to pick up her kid."

"Did she leave," Father Joe's hands were in his pockets. He rocked back and forth, trying to be casual. "With that man?"

The bartender gave the slightest nod.

By the time Father Joe got back to the car, Bear had a plan. "We're gonna park at the library," he said. "You and me are going to walk every street between the library and the bar, and then we're going to walk every street between the library and the car."

He bent his head and looked sideways at Father Joe. His ski cap was now on and pulled low on his forehead. His ponytail hung down his back. "Remember, Father, you gotta kinda relax if you want to find things. You can't be all hunched over." He imitated Father Joe in his normal posture. "You gotta, you know, loosen up." He shook his hands as if to demonstrate how it was done. "She's gonna come to us."

The night felt like a cold, shallow pool. The light from the streetlamps yellowed the ice on the sidewalks, now covered with a shim of snow. They started walking systematically, on the grid of the city blocks, turning down alleys, behind old brick buildings, next to the hulking beasts of dumpsters, past a motel with five-dollar-an-hour rooms. No one was out on the streets, though some of the bars were lit up and had customers. Father Joe poked his head inside each one and looked around. No Sally. No cowboy hat. Father Joe felt not one ounce of confidence that Bear's plan would work. But since he had no other plan, he tried to do this one with fidelity. Integrity. Like Veronica's spiderweb.

The night stretched endlessly. He thought of Alice and Rowena in the car. Would they walk until morning? How far into this night did Bear's plan extend? Did integrity mean a whole night of walking? Where had the woman gone? Why had she forgotten her daughter? They should leave her and take her daughter to Windy Creek. Let that be a lesson to her. Then he remembered how both times he had seen her, her face had lit up at her daughter's name or face. And the daughter too—she lit up in the presence of her mother.

Father Joe didn't know how much time had passed when they found themselves in an alley with a parking ramp on one side and a small row of glass doors on the other. No lamps lit this alley, but their eyes had now adjusted to the dark. As before, they simply walked and listened.

The pile did not at first appear to be a person. It appeared as a lump of darkness on the snow, perhaps a stray black coat, abandoned. But as they walked closer, the pile moved slightly, and they stopped. Bear bent down first. He pulled back the coat to reveal a tangle of black hair and Sally's face. He looked up at Father Joe to ask what didn't need to be asked. She was unconscious. There was a small spray of vomit near her, and one of her eyes looked cracked underneath with a trickle of dried blood.

Together they scooped her up. Bear took her shoulders, Father Joe her legs. She was awkwardly positioned between them and continued to stir. Father Joe's back ached, and he wondered how many steps he could go. As if reading his mind, Bear said, "I got her, Father." They set her down on the snow, and Bear pulled the woman into his arms and carried her into the light on the street.

"Should we call the police?" Father Joe said. "The hospital?"

"Let's ask mom," Bear said.

Alice had seen them coming and was already out of the car.

"Spread her on the back seat," she said. "Bear, let's use your jacket as a pillow. Father, do you keep a blanket in the trunk? I'll sit back here with her. You three up front. Let's go."

———

In the silence through which they drove—out past the lights of the city, into the dark highway rarely brightened by other headlights—the children fell asleep. Father Joe looked into the rearview mirror at the two women in the back. Alice held Sally's head in her lap and was looking down on her like she might have looked at one of her own daughters. It might have been Jackie's broken face or Marlena's stubborn one. She stroked the woman's face as if she were entering a dream.

Father Joe watched as Alice actively forged truth with her own hands, bending the will of the stars to her own will.

As they crossed the Missouri at Chamberlin, Alice began to sing, at first almost inaudibly, but growing louder. The song had the wind in it. It had the river in it. It had every child lost, and every single one found. The sound had the way that Alice drew things together. "One of ours," it said. Every living thing into one garment, each bead connected to every other bead.

If I could translate this, Father Joe thought, it might be:

Do not hand over the life of your dove to wild beasts.
Do not forget the lives of your poor forever.

But those lines didn't quite have the wind in them. Alice's singing and the psalm were not a perfect match. Alice had entered a place where she had taken up embroidery with the stars themselves. It was a place far away and impossibly close at hand. It was not a place Father Joe knew how to get to.

Father Joe realized that he had not prayed since he had found the letters. Somehow the letters had opened up a distance between himself and prayer, and he had not even tried to cross it. But now, in the dark and quiet of the car, accompanied by Alice's song and the sleeping children, he tried to pray. *Help them.*

His prayer was the lightest possible touch, like the brush of a feather. Then gone.

26

All Parts Away

Dear ~~Bishop Reginald~~ Ronald,

I am writing to inform you of my resignation, effective as of Easter Monday, April 23, 1984.

It is my intention to leave the office of the priesthood. I believe that the attached letters should give you a strong enough sense of my reasons. Yes, they are more than ten years old, and I have been holding on to them for quite some time, a fact that I have had difficulty explaining to myself. I suppose it is because I believed, on some level, that we were doing some good here.

Have you ever read Lame Deer's vision, when he imagines the "white man's world" rolled up like a carpet? I sometimes dream that too. That we, and our apparatus, all our structures and files and the circus of our comings and goings, would fold up like tents and wander off, leaving behind the great, pristine, vast wilderness of this strange place and its strange light and its people who have held on to that strangeness against all odds.

But the cost has been great and that remains a fantasy. I have no strong sense of what good leaving will do.

It causes me great pain to say, but I still feel I must say, that I have made copies of these letters, and I am prepared to send them to the tribal council, the Rapid City Sentinel, the Argus

Leader in Sioux Falls, and the Minneapolis Star and Tribune.
But I have decided to refrain from doing so for the time being
because... because... because...

~~*I want to give you a chance.*~~

~~*I am a coward.*~~

~~*What good would it do?*~~ *What good would it do? I mean that*
quite literally. What good? That's what I am waiting to know. I
want to know what good can be made or done.

Also, I am taking the diocesan car. I will return it eventually.

Sincerely,

~~Father Kreitzer~~

~~Kreitzer~~

Joe

They'd arrived back on Windy Creek after midnight. Marlena
had heard their car on the snow-packed gravel and turned on
the porch light to greet them. They'd made beds on the living
room floor. Sally had become restless and was thrashing a little.
Alice brought her some water in a Mason jar and smoothed a
hand across her forehead. Rowena scooted closer to her and put
a hand on her shoulder. That soothed her. Father Joe returned to
the rectory feeling like he had lived a thousand years since he'd
left it that morning.

He didn't go to bed. Instead he sat and composed the letter
that he had been writing in his mind. He didn't know when, he
didn't even know if, he would send it. But he felt clarity emerg-
ing, like a grain of crystal—one hard, flat surface.

At the beginning of Lent, Alice and Father Joe were in the sacristy
packing up the brass candelabra and the not-yet-consecrated oil,
the butts of candles and the statues that people had given to the

church over the years. They packed up patens and cloths, silver polish, and incense. Most of it would go into storage at Blessed Sacrament.

Sally and Rowena were still with Alice. When Sally had awakened on Windy Creek, she was not as angry as Alice had expected her to be. In drunkenness, Windy Creek was the last place she wanted to be, but in sobriety, she stepped out on Alice's porch to feel the wind. She walked down in Alice's boots to the creek and stood along the icy bank. She hadn't asked to go out to her grandmother's place, and Alice hadn't suggested it. Now she was watching the slow ascent of spring come to the reservation.

"I've decided against Hastings," Father Joe said as he wrapped a set of candlesticks in newspaper.

"That so," Alice said. She was standing at an angle to him, and she turned to look at him over her shoulder. He kept focused on the box in front of him.

"It's not for me."

Where does all this go? Father Joe wondered. Objects. Statues. Here was a Sacred Heart of Jesus. Here was a statue of St. Francis with a broken foot. Blessed things. You can't throw them away, and you can't keep them either. He felt like they should put it all out in front of the church and let people carry it away. Anything the people didn't want didn't need to be kept. But that wasn't how it worked. Canon law dictated how it would work exactly. He expected to get some paperwork in the mail that would give him the exact shutting-down procedure. They'd developed these rituals over several hundred years. They'd have it down pat.

"What will you do?"

"That part I haven't exactly figured out yet," he said. "Maybe they could store me in a reliquary like this statue." He held up the St. Francis.

"Oh, Father. You know, I told you, you are always welcome with me."

Former priest as vagabond. Well, why not? He laughed a little at the thought that he could become one of the people randomly sleeping on Alice's floor, and a new priest, coming by with reserved sacrament, would have to see him there. This wasn't so far out of the realm of possibility, he realized, given the direction of his thoughts.

He knew he was waiting for word from Veronica. He could feel the waiting, like his head was tilted in a particular direction toward the wind, waiting for birdsong. He wouldn't call it a summons, exactly, but supposed it was. He wanted to keep that possibility open as long as he could. Where was she? What if she didn't write in time and he was already gone? And suppose he never heard from her again. That was possible too. Then what would he do? He had never, he recognized, faced this kind of uncertainty. He had always been told exactly where to go and where to be. The choice to say no to Hastings and not even to negotiate for something else opened up an entire field of choice. He felt that field like a great wrenching in his guts. Desire and fear mixed up together. But the bishop still thought he was going to Hastings, so that was also possible with only the slightest motion on Joe's part.

"Remember Bear has a check-in on Thursday with the court," Alice said. "I'm going to bring Sally."

He looked up. "Why are you bringing Sally?"

"I'm just giving you fair warning," she said.

The postcard arrived. There was a picture of a desert canyon, the red sun casting shadows on the canyon floor. On the back, the loops of Veronica's handwriting. He remembered how concerned he had been that Jolene at the post office not know about their correspondence, and now the postcard arrived open and plain.

Dear Joseph,

I can't help but think: What if you came? Write to the brothers at Christ in the Desert Monastery. They will let me know.

V

P.S. "All parts away for the progress of souls."—Walt Whitman

---

A V with a loop at the top, a soft curve at the bottom, a lift like a bird in flight. *What if you came?* He wondered what she imagined and what she was doing with the brothers at Christ in the Desert. It wasn't an invitation. It wasn't a summons. It left all doors open. *All parts away for the progress of souls.*

27

Double Vision

ON WEDNESDAY NIGHT, Bear knocked on the door of the rectory. His dark hair curled across his forehead, pulled back glossy into a wavy ponytail behind his head. He stood with a bit of a hunch, and when Father Joe ushered him inside the kitchen door, he shuffled with his footsteps, as if he hadn't gotten used to his height or adjusted his stride to the length of his legs.

Even so, to Father Joe, he looked like a man, or like the man was hiding behind the boy who had not yet shaved the mustache growing on his upper lip or the thin skim of dark hair now on his cheeks.

"I been thinking about something," he started when they sat at the table. He kept his old brown coat on with his hands shoved deep in the pockets. "You and my mom. You don't ever ask about that night."

"Do you want to tell me about it?" Just say the words straight, Joe. No striving. Keep your hope for the boy out of your voice.

"I don't know if I do or not. That's the problem." He pulled a hand out of his pocket and ran a fingernail in the groove along the edge of the table.

"I just went over to check on Jackie. It's . . . I knew what he was like. I didn't trust him, but I didn't think."

He glanced up, as if to gauge Father Joe's interest, to see if he was listening. "Do you ever? Do you ever see things, like, in two parts?"

Father Joe leaned forward and crossed his hands in front of him on the table. "I'm not sure what you mean."

The boy laughed. It had a bit of a hollow sound, not joyful. He shook his head. "Like one minute you see something the way everybody tells you it is. And then for a second you see the same thing, but this time different, like, like . . ." He returned his hand to his pocket and started bouncing his leg up and down. "Like it's all connected."

Father Joe sat still like you might if you were waiting for an animal to emerge out of the woods. He dared not even breathe.

"That night, I don't even know who grabbed the knife. When I got there he was already drunk. He didn't see me. I was outside. I heard a crash. It wasn't self-defense, Father, like the lawyer wants me to say. I wasn't even protecting her. She was already lying on the floor bleeding, and I didn't know if she was dead or what. He . . . He wasn't even in the same room with her. I wanted to hurt him, like he was the one who killed Albert. Like it was his fault. I did. I am not sure I ever wanted anything that bad."

He squeezed his eyes shut like he was trying to block out some light.

"It was right then that I had that double vision. Like I was me but not me. And in myself, but not.

"I don't regret it. I don't. I can't because it was like I was there and I wasn't there. And he was. His knife was. But my mom."

Tears were close by, but he was shutting them off, holding them tightly inside himself.

"She's hurting so much. And it's my fault. I did it."

He put his arms out on the table, straight, like an ablution. His long, graceful fingers spread out on the table like he was reaching for something. Then he rested his head on his arms and started to shake. Father Joe reached out and put a hand on his head.

After a few minutes, he sat up. He was still shaking, but trying to get a hold of himself, so his words came out tight.

"I've still been seeing things that way. Not all the time, but sometimes. Like there's the me with my feet on the ground and then there's the me flying around above. Gayle says it means something. He says it's a special thing. But I think maybe I just broke myself somehow. I might just be broken."

At the word "broken," he wept. Finally, he spoke very softly. "I should just tell them. I'll just say 'I did it. I stabbed him.' And then the two parts will come together, and they'll send me away, and that will be better for everybody."

Father Joe sighed. "Let's not get carried away, Bear. We've got to get through this check-in, and we can talk things over with the lawyer tomorrow. Your mom needs you by her side every minute that you can be there."

The boy roused. Father Joe handed him his handkerchief. "It's a clean one," he said. Bear blew his nose. He was embarrassed, Father Joe could tell. He hadn't meant to break down, as if to prove his own words against himself.

"You know," Father Joe said, "this business about being broken. That's the thing nobody tells you. We're all broken. I'm broken. Your mom's broken. Vincent is broken. Albert was broken. You can't really get through this life without it. But I think you should listen to Gayle. He might just know what he's talking about. Gayle knows about broken things."

"I don't think Rowena is broken."

"You might be right about that." Joe laughed. "She might not be broken. Yet."

Old men leaned listlessly against the tribal building in the sunshine. Crows poked at the ground around the dumpster. The day was unseasonably warm, and they tracked mud in with their boots from the unpaved parking lot.

They sat on the benches in the paneled courtroom: Sally next to Rowena next to Bear next to Alice next to Father Joe. The lawyer had come in from Rapid City in his Honda. He looked pressed and polished, like he was ready to do some business.

Father Joe wondered about all the oak in the courtroom. Oak was supposed to convey a sense of solidity and finality. The great oaks of righteousness. We are firm in our foundation. Where had they cut the trees that paneled this courtroom and had been shaped into tables and chairs and benches? Father Joe wondered. That was the kind of question that Alice would ask. Whose trees were supposed to be conveying what justice to them?

Bear's leg jumped up and down, shaking the whole row, until Alice put a hand on it.

"Your Honor," the lawyer said when it was their turn. "We have new information in the case of Bernard Nighthawk."

The judge looked down at them over his glasses.

"We have Bernard's biological mother in the courtroom with us today, ready to testify as to Bernard's origins."

Alice was staring steadily ahead. Father Joe felt the urge to turn toward her. "This woman." The lawyer gestured at Sally. "Sally Campbell is Bernard Nighthawk's biological mother. She is a member of the Lakota Sioux Tribe. Therefore we ask the court to rule that the case of Bernard Nighthawk remain in tribal court."

"Birth certificate?"

"We have no birth certificate. As we initially suspected, Miss Campbell gave birth outside of any hospital facility and did not register the birth with any entity."

"By what means have you then determined that Miss Campbell is Bernard Nighthawk's biological mother?"

"Her testimony, Your Honor, which she will give to the court today. And we have a handwriting expert, your honor, who has certified that the handwriting on the original note is, in fact, Sally Campbell's handwriting." He handed over a paper to the clerk, who handed it to the judge.

The perfect B. This was Alice's doing. There was no doubt about it. That handwriting was shared by all the nun-trained girls. They hadn't "determined" that Sally was Bear's mother; Alice had decided it. If the court needed proof, then she was happy to provide it.

This was the "fair warning." What Alice had meant was: "You are going to keep your mouth shut, Father." He felt a little burst of anger at her, accompanied by a small amount of awe. Alice hadn't told him because she didn't want to turn him into a conspirator. Here was a truth sharp and bitter: no one had told him. But this was what Alice did. This is what she had been doing that very night when he drove them to Windy Creek together. If Bear needed a mother, then by God, she would give him a mother. She could sing a mother into being. Now that was power.

The judge looked at the paper in his hands. He cleared his throat. He looked down at other papers lying nearby as if trying to refresh himself on the particulars. Father Joe studied him. He was a few years younger than Joe himself, and Joe remembered that less than a year before, he had spent a night in jail in a power struggle with the tribal council. In a surreal turn of events—all justice on the reservation struck Father Joe as surreal—he was back on the bench. Here he was, the only native judge on the reservation, Ivy League educated, trying to mix the best of both worlds and ending up with the worst in front of him day after day. Father Joe felt for him.

"Did you abandon this child?" The judge summoned Sally toward him. Sally rose. She looked tiny in this room with its large imposing furniture, like she was a broken branch of the oak tree.

"I was homeless at the time," she said softly. "I didn't have any way to care for him."

"Speak up."

"I said, I was homeless."

"Where's the boy's father?"

"I don't know."

"The court can't hear you."

"I don't know."

"What is the father's name?"

"I don't know." Sally's voice had gotten louder as it had gotten tighter.

The judge turned to the lawyer as if he should know something about the boy's father.

"How is it that we don't have a paternal identification?"

"The mother states that she does not know the identity of the father."

"How is that possible?"

There was a long and awkward silence as everyone in the courtroom worked out an answer to the judge's question. Each kept their own confidence. Sally looked down.

The judge sighed and looked out at the room. "The court will study this new evidence and determine next steps."

Outside the courtroom, they stood in a scattered cluster. Father Joe felt like it was possible they would go on like this forever. Another court date and then another one, with no ruling ever made and no final judgment. At some point, would it cease to matter what the crime had even been? What Bear had done or not done? What his reasons were, in the moment, after the moment?

The lawyer ushered Alice and Bear over to a corner. Father Joe glanced at them on their hard plastic chairs. Bear sprawled, his legs wide and arms crossed, like he'd already given up on whatever the lawyer was saying. Alice scowled, sitting up very straight.

On the phone, Father Joe gave Brother Ezekiel the details, trying not to think too hard about what the man made of the situation.

He would arrive in Chama, he said, on the Wednesday after Easter. If he could please tell Veronica Foster, who he believed was staying with them. "Yes, of course!" The brother was entirely too cheerful.

A week later, another postcard, this one SUNRISE IN THE DESERT.

Wednesday, April 25, 5 p.m.. Fina's. Chama, New Mexico
The same beautiful V.

A P.S. would have been nice. He felt vaguely irritated by the mystery of it all. The unspoken.

————————

On the Monday of Holy Week, they were summoned back to the court. There was no more testimony. No trial. No more dates. Bear had pleaded guilty. The judge made his ruling while they sat in the courtroom, and Bear stood with the lawyer at the table in front of the bench.

"In light of the severity of the crime, and the fact that the boy, Bernard Nighthawk, has confessed to stabbing Vincent Bordeaux, albeit in an act of self-defense, as he claims, it is the determination of the court that the defendant spend six months at the State Training School in Plankinton. When he returns to the custody of his mother in September, the court rules that the parties return to this courtroom for a custodial plan that is agreeable to all parties."

Alice started forward. The lawyer laid a hand on her arm. It was the best that they could hope for, his hand said.

"Young man." The judge turned to Bernard. "Make good use of this time apart from your family to reflect on the life you want to lead."

There was a lie at the root of it. No child had ever returned from Plankinton more whole.

28

The Road Out

THE ROAD OUT from Windy Creek was muddy and slushy in the dark of the early spring morning. When he reached the highway, it was solid again. He reached the Nebraska border as the sun rose and drove the roller coaster south through the pale hills. Chama was out there somewhere. Over some mountains. Along a river. A place called Fina's. Veronica.

He drove as the land turned red. The Rockies lurked in front of him like hulking bodies lying end to end on the horizon. The road was so deserted that he felt like he was driving from one no place to another no place with nothing in between. But then Denver appeared on the horizon and he stopped to eat a hamburger. He drove into the mountains, across a treeless expanse where antelope spread out. He saw their pale bodies behind fence posts, defying the boundaries laid out by the region's ranchers. Indifferent really. They mingled with cattle as if visiting the neighbors, their effervescent bodies all but translucent against the heaviness of the cows.

He pulled over and slept. He hadn't slept at all the night before leaving. He'd gone over and over in his mind the gestures of departure, like rehearsing for a play. He'd determined not to see anyone. He didn't want any long goodbyes with Alice or with anyone else. They'd closed and locked St. Rose's door together, and then there was nothing to say. He wanted to believe that she knew everything he couldn't say. *There is no speech or language.*

When he woke up, he felt like he'd passed through some kind of veil and his mind was only on the road ahead of him. What lay there. Something he wanted so badly he was willing to give up his whole life for it. Sell all that he had, as it were. Although it wasn't. He had nothing, nothing that was his own. Even the car was stolen. Borrowed. On loan. Then why the dread?

The landscape became dominated by the mountains on the horizon. The land of Windy Creek had only two dimensions: earth and sky. Here there were more layers: grassland and foot-hills and the rocky expanses beyond them, the place where the trees stopped growing and where clouds gathered. He felt at moments suffocated. Where was his horizon? The mountains cut off his view of the sky.

The farther he drove, the more he could feel the civilization changing. He recognized the all-but-abandoned trailers and the occasional shack where inhabitants made little of their own presence. He knew the weather-tortured farm implements and the fences in disrepair. But soon enough there were other signs. An adobe church. A window in rock. Words on signs in Spanish. In the branches of the occasional tree you could see the nests of birds of prey. He wondered if they were red-tailed hawks.

He felt like he was in one of the old Westerns from his child-hood that he watched in the dark of a movie theater in Pierre. Men on horseback amid sagebrush, chasing and being chased. He'd understood then: this is about me and this is not about me. He began to feel that the light was changing—or maybe that everything was becoming less earth and more light.

There were still patches of snow along the Conejos River, and there were sheep grazing next to the abandoned bones of an old Catholic church. Willows grew thickly beside the road, ready to burst into green. On the mountain pass before Chama, the road turned muddy again and slush brushed the Buick. Willows gave way to scrub oak.

WELCOME TO CHAMA, the sign said, although no town appeared immediately. There was an abandoned railroad with old steam engines sulking next to rotting wood barns. There was a river that flowed toward the Monastery of Christ in the Desert, somewhere south of where Father Joe was. He wondered if Fina's would be easy to find. He found he couldn't think about the particulars. There was no rehearsal that he could bring to mind. There was a blank.

He parked among a preponderance of buildings painted a variety of pinks—rose petal pink, pale pink, deep pink almost tending toward orange. Some of the pink was nearly gray. He noticed how close together the buildings and houses were compared to Windy Creek, where everything was scattered as if flung. Here there was more of a town: streets and cross streets, houses built one after another in rows. He put on a stocking cap in the sharp wind and walked on a decaying sidewalk. Eventually he saw a sign for Fina's. There were a few people about. More cowboy hats than he'd expected, the lined faces of farmers and ranchers. The people had a weather-beaten look about them that reminded him of Windy Creek and made him feel at home.

Veronica was standing by the long nose of a Datsun in the gravel parking lot of Fina's. She'd been watching him walk up the road and was smiling. "It's you!" she said with a wide grin. "I can't believe you came!" Her hair was blowing in the wind. She wore a dress the same color as the pale green hills through which he'd just driven. She looked . . . he wondered what the right word was. He didn't want to project his own longings onto her. Free. She looked free. Like whatever she was searching for, she hadn't exactly found it, but the looking had been good for her.

She turned toward the mud of the car and laughed. "The drive up from the monastery was rough," she said. "I almost didn't make it. No one told me what it is like around here in spring.

One long mud pit and the poor car bouncing from one side of the road to the other. How was your drive?"

"Long," he said, rubbing his eyes. "Strange. Beautiful. Like entering another world."

"Isn't the light here wonderful?" she said. "I feel like I've almost been doing nothing but studying the light since I came."

She looked at him with gentleness. "Thank you for coming," she said. "I know it's all a bit . . . dramatic."

The sparkle of her had taken him aback a little. He wanted to ask about it. Where had it come from? When had it come? She looked like she was emanating the same light that she was talking about.

Fina's was a tiny café, and when Joe studied the menu, he felt baffled. The waitress said her name was Maria-Elena and did he want green chili on his enchiladas. He glanced at Veronica for help.

"You at least have to try it," she said, laughing. "Say on the side."

"I don't know what I'm doing here."

She laughed. "In more ways than one."

She was teaching English to the monks, she told him, who came from all over the world. The monastery had just been received into the English Province of the Subiaco Congregation, she said, as a conventual priory.

"What in the world," said Joe. "I'm embarrassed to say that I don't know what any of that means. I should."

"It's a Benedictine thing," she said. "I think Italian basically. But they needed English teachers, and I thought, 'Why not?' They have a little guesthouse for me. Except for classes, we're mostly silent. I do most of my communicating these days by smiling. And I'm writing and studying. I meet with one of the monks regularly to talk about free will." She laughed. "Ironic, I know. I don't know how long I'll stay, but for now, it's perfect."

"I don't know what I pictured," Joe said. "Maybe I pictured you living like a hippie in a tent or sleeping in your car or hanging out by the ocean like a teenager. I hadn't even thought of New Mexico."

"I know. When I wrote to you, I truly had no idea where I was going. I just knew that I had to go. Then I saw a little advertisement for English teachers, and I thought 'That's it!'"

After they ate, they walked through the neighborhoods of Chama. Father Joe was surprised by the number of Marys in improvised caves. For a long time, they didn't speak. They walked as if accustoming themselves to the sound of the other's footsteps, listening to the wind meet the trees.

"I have the urge to keep walking," Joe said finally. "Up and up into these hills and then into mountains. Where would I end up?"

"Pagosa Springs," she said, and laughed.

"What now?" They'd been walking in the dark for some time.

"I thought maybe . . ." Veronica stopped walking and turned to him. She took both of his hands in hers and looked up into his face. "I thought maybe you would spend the night with me."

"I have let go of that," he said. "You don't have to do or be anything for me."

"I know, Joseph," she said. "I know." Her eyes filled with tears for a moment and she blinked them away.

They walked back to the Buick, and he drove them to a neon sign. ELKHORN LODGE. He found the office and came back with a key. In front of a little cabin with a porch light on, they paused and sat in the near dark.

"I haven't been able to picture this at all," he said.

"There are no words," she said.

"No," he said. "I still don't have any words." They opened their doors simultaneously. He opened the door to their room and turned on the light. Then he turned it off again as she came in behind him.

Touch arriving—sweet—no less for its late arrival.

The next evening, they pulled lawn chairs from Veronica's Datsun and sat in the motel parking lot facing west toward the mountains.

"Just watch now," Veronica said. "Pay attention. Have you ever watched a complete sunset? Here's what I've noticed: it takes a long, long time for the darkness to overcome the light. You almost can't say exactly when it happens. There's a light show, all the color, but then there's this gradual fading while the stars come out."

"Okay," he said. "Let's stay until it is completely dark."

They were silent, watching the pink and tangerine quicken around them and the scrub grass of the motel lawn bathe in rose light.

"What are you going to do now?" Veronica asked at last.

"I don't know. I abandoned them—the people that I was a part of. You know that about me, right? You know that I just left them there. But going back. That's not an option." *Father-of-what*, he thought. Albert had guessed from the beginning.

"I've been thinking about that line that you sent on your post-card," Joe said. "'All parts away for the progress of souls.' And also a line from *The Cloud of Unknowing*. Have you ever read that? It goes, 'God will provide for those who make no account or provision for themselves.' That's certainly where I've gotten. No account or provision."

"A wandering holy man? Isn't that a stage of life in Hinduism? What's it called—where old men start forest wandering?"

"I don't know about the holy part. I might skip that. I think it might be good if I didn't know who I was for a while."

"Didn't Tolstoy end his days as a wandering monk?"

He looked at her slyly. The side of her face, the high cheek-bone, the lilt of her eyebrow made him as happy as it ever had. "Are you saying that my idea is cliché?"

"Not at all." She laughed. "I'm saying that it has precedent." She reached over and took his hand.

The letters sat in the back of his car in their manila cocoon.

She looked toward the glow in the sky behind the western mountain.

"You'll have to return the car, I suppose."

"I will," he said.

"But not yet."

"No," he said. His heart lifted. "Not yet."

Acknowledgments

THE DIOCESAN LETTERS represented in this novel are based, in part, on historical letters that former students and survivors brought to light in 2011 from the St. Francis Mission School on the Rosebud Indian Reservation in South Dakota. You can find out more from the Boarding School Healing Project at https://boardingschoolhealing.org/.

The story of this book begins with two remarkable children. One of them I understood immediately: she loved books. The other I couldn't make a lot of sense of, but I knew one thing: his sketchbook was a lifeline for him in difficult circumstances. These two children, who are now adults with children of their own, stayed with me over the years of writing this book, and I am grateful to both of them.

At the end of the process, I am grateful to Jim McCoy, Maya Torrez, and the wonderful team at the University of Iowa Press, who have seen it to completion and brought it out into the world. I am grateful to Wendy Levinson, my agent, who is perhaps the fiercest and most loving companion this book has ever had.

The others to whom I owe gratitude are legion: Clyde Edgerton pulled the manuscript out of the drawer and showed me a better way; Darrow Woods took a long walk with me at a critical moment; Jamie Arnold, Joanne Greenberg, Diane Mott Davidson, and Marilyn Saltzman were the book's first community and shared its highs and lows, and Hebrew, with me; my Leadville book group read at least two versions of this manuscript and Susan Fishman I think read three; many years ago a woman at the Lakota Language Department at Sinte Gleska University sat with a stranger and corrected her Lakota with grace, although all errors are mine alone; Sam Frykholm traveled with me to South Dakota and concluded that I needed to rename most of my characters; Peter Frykholm companioned me at all stages; my sister, Sarah Hankerson, reminded me that not having a strong grasp on reality can be a benefit to a novelist; my brother, Jason Johnson, has offered many times to house and feed a starving artist; my parents, Tom and Michele Johnson, said, "Do what you love"; Amie Adams and Lil Copan each spoke important words at the right moment. Mara Naselli has sustained a life-long conversation.

And finally, Kirsten Sampera believed and believed and believed.